MEN IN MY BED

TRUE LOVE IS HARD TO FIND

BY MERCURIES RYZEN

RELATIONSHIP CHRONICLES

ISBN: 978-1-943409-66-2

Table of Contents

Introduction

There was a time when I would wake up to the noise of the city streets. Cars were passing by and people were honking their horns, yelling for a taxi cab to stop, and just plain noise. There's not much joy in that kind of waking startling noise. Yet, the sounds of the country are more inviting. The rooster crows just before sunrise, and the dogs barked as people pass by going to work or school and you still feel like staying in bed. Sunshine is beaming in the bedroom window, bouncing off the wallpaper, and you can smell the coffee brewing on the stove and the biscuits in the oven. Great grandmother is up before sunrise. It was a wonderful experience to live with my great grandmother in the South in the 1960s.

Things were happening, but as a child, my sister Joyce and I did not pay much attention to what was going on. We played, eat, shit, and slept in that order. Bad things happened to other people in the world and us. The color seemed to be a great concern and respect, make sure to answer "Yes Sir" and "Yes Mam." We stayed out of grown folk's conversations, held our heads down when spoken to, out of respect. Never look a grown person in the eyes, stare them down, a whipping was waiting. However, "Why" were always in the forefront of my mind, but it never left my lips. I was usually close enough to hear what was being said, eavesdropping. I would sit in the closet, in a clothesline in the bedroom, so heavy with clothes you could not be seen. Sometimes I would fall asleep, only to wake to great grandmother calling out my name, "Shasha, come on now, time to eat."

Dinner was always, and I mean, always homemade from scratch, I loved watching her cook our meals. Mash potatoes with real butter and cream, fried chicken back, I hated the Bunkie on my chicken so she would cut the Bunkie off. I was dead sure dodo was going to come out. Whatever we were eating for dinner, rice was included, making sure our stomach was heavy.

Cousin Dewey would come for a visit. He lived in the community but not the neighborhood. Our house sat alone, surrounded by a forest and a graveyard. Cousin Dewey was a "bad" old man that made my bones painful. No one, not even the doctors knew what was wrong. But the days passed by, and I actually felt worse for the other people in the world more so than for myself. Watching the Horry of War on T.V., Presidents assassinated, and Martin Luther King was dead. People did not want people to help. I heard what was going on in the world, but my world was becoming just as unbearable.

I knew how to Pray, we were always in Church, "all day long," and sometimes during the wee hours of the night. I can recall saying, "When I grow up, I am never going to Church all day." In my world, I prayed that 'God will kill old man Dewey. I prayed for a lot of killing from six years old to ten years old. I never took any of my prayer requests to God back. I prayed that someone would love me. For some reason, I felt like I did not belong to this family. I did not look like them, I did not act or behave like them, and I was not treated as my sister.

My hair turned from black to clay red, maybe because of the old man Dewey or a million other reasons. My reasoning behind the color change is too much to think about. What old man Dewey was doing to me was changing my mind. I found myself picking the hair out of the top of my head while sitting in class with my overcoat on in the middle of summertime, it felt so well, and I wondered why. After pulling out one strain, I picked another and another, then white stuff off of the hair root. Then I would tie a bunch of hair together and put it in one of my class books. I thought no more pulling my hair for that day, and often days would go by, that was free of hair-pulling.

 Alone at school, I looked out the door as the other children played in a circle, and all fall down. It seemed like a fun game, but I did not fit. The little girls would ask me to play, but I was shy and stayed away. My clothes were as pretty as theirs, and they liked what I wore, but I just could not bring myself to play. Tragic things were all around me, and it could be because of what old man Dewey was doing to me. I did not think to tell anyone, but God, and I knew he listened to my Prayer. I said my *Our Father* prayer every night, I did my cutchie bow every night, and I mispronounced my words to the prayer, but God understood me. Great grandmother tried to find out what was happening, and she kept me in the doctor's office. Doctor Mays was his name, our family physician that made house visits at any hour. He told Great grandmother, "She will grow out of it soon. The way he looked at me and into my eyes, I knew he knew what was happening. "Keep a close eye on her," he said a close eye.

 Great grandmother did not know how to braid hair, so she gave us two or three plats, one in the top and one on each side of our head. Our hair was okay, other kids at the bus stop were worse off. You see, the bus stop was another ordeal. My sister Joyce and I stood away from the other children. They made "fun" of our New York intonations and pulled our hair just to hear us curse. They pulled on our New York clothes, tore our stockings, and exposed our griddle all before arriving at school. No one to tell, so we fought back with cursing until we realized that is what they wanted. They wanted to hear two little city girls cursing in the country.

The school was a trying place, and I noticed a few of the other kids in my class going through stuff. Sandra, for instance, her mother died when she was in the second grade in my homeroom class. Her mother was killed by her father, and Sandra was a beautiful little girl. She was as tall as I and I was tall, and my shoes were a size seven in the second grade. Sandra had long, flowing, thick curly red hair that stopped at her butt. The teachers always talked about her hair, and I admired her red hair wondering if Cousin Dewey visits her in the night. But, after her mother died,

Sandra was no more Sandra. She went to say with her grandmother down the road from our house, and she was never the same, not even her hair. All her hair was gone. It went from being as long as my arm to as short as my little toe. I remember Sandra. She seemed worse than me.

The school was still a trying place. My second-grade teacher, Mrs. White, died. She went fishing one day and was bitten by an Eel, and Mrs. White died. Oh, I was so sad, I loved Mrs. White she was good to me, and she would let me write my name between two lines. On the practice paper, I had perfect penmanship, I could read well, and I was attentive. I missed Mrs. White, and I thought about her a lot. Some teachers are like the mothers that are not at home. This was Mrs. White for me. Don't get me wrong, I love my Great grandmother, and she was the best in my World. She did everything with us; she kept us busy. I believe that our activities with great-grand-mother helped me to be sane. We never planned anything to do; we just did — fishing under the railroad track, where the Train would pass a few times during the daylight hours. Great grandmother must have known the schedule because we were never caught on the tracks. I did not care for putting the worm on the hock, but I would tie the neck bone to the fishing pole and dangle it in the murky waters until something nibbled at the meat. Coming to my rescue was my little sister Joyce with the dip net, caught fish and crabs all at once. I think for every bad memory, great grandmother created at least two good memories.

Quilting was a highly acclaimed experience with great grandmother. My sister Joyce and I were to cut out the squares evenly from old clothing we no longer wore. Nothing was ever thrown away. She showed us how to needle stitch the squares together, and then, she would follow with the stumble and a needle making smaller stitches. This quilting ordeal lasted for *months' hands can't go but so fast*. We were allowed to use sharp scissors and needles. Great grandmother used Crocker sackcloth for the lining that was afterward covered with a smoother material, linen-like. Once you got to lay between the quilt and the sheets, you could bet your bottom dollar. You could not move. This was our heat in the winter, could not leave a cast iron stove burning in a shotgun house overnight. You were sure to burn by the next morning to a crisp. You had to keep turning the ashes until all the smoke or sign of fire life was gone. If you see smoke, there is fire.

Oh boy, as a little girl, I knew I was different from most little girls in our neighborhood. I wanted ten children from ten different men just to see what they would look like. I believed if a boy kissed me, we were then married. I liked to play house with my little sister Joyce, and we took the animals around the house as our children; chickens, pigs, cats, and dogs. However, I only thought this way when I was in the country with my great grandmother. When in Brooklyn, New York, my thought patterns were much more different. I wondered how can I get to the pizza parlor and spend these twenty cents on one slice of pizza or run behind the ice cream truck without my mother missing me.

So, I could get to the pizza parlor unnoticed, I walked a long stretch of sidewalk from Hopkinson avenue and turned left on Pikins avenue, and there it was pizza. I could smell it from so far away. I stepped up to the pizza window, hand him my 20 cents, and he cut what seems to be such a long slice that it covered both of my hands as I held the wax paper. The pizza man dressed in his white hat and chef jacket made sure I did not mess up my dress or burn my small delicate hands. The cheese pulled off the crust so long with the first hot bite. In no hurry to get back home, I walked the streets listening to the music playing "on Broadway," seeing the men and young boys crowded around a barrel playing some sort of card trick game and shooting craps in the corner. I stopped by Pop's store for a Twinkie and pineapple soda, I know it was less than twenty-five cents. Pop's store was really close to the apartment building, and I proceed on my slow stroll home. At the age of six, I was more like a twelve-year-old. I watched the street sweeper clean the street back and forth, kids playing hopscotch, double Dutch, and riding homemade go-carts made out of soda crates. Young trees were planted in front of each building with wiring tied to each side to keep it in place and straight. The neighborhood was a joy to live in, but the inside of the apartment building was a different story. My family, Scott's, was well known from the top floor to the bottom. My grandmother Roberta lived on the second floor; she was at the time perceived as the wicked witch. Hateful as the stink smell of shit, never really saw her smile much. She loves to look good, glamorous, long weave hanging to her shoulders, chocolate brown with bronze highlights in the front, and a touch on the sides. Updated and stylish clothing, shoes, and handbags, everything came in a big beautiful round box. She shopped like she had money. I remember this suit, baby pink, soft wool-like a down blanket that stopped at her knees with a long shawl to match and at the end of the shawl mink like fur and the shoes were to die for, wicker with a cross strap that she pulled up over her heels accompanied with a wicker box handbag. She was a beautiful, tall, slim woman with the completion of dark mahogany. Roberta was a perfect size five as if she had never given birth to any children. Meanwhile, living in the apartment with my sister Joyce and I was my uncle Lonnie, Uncle Junior, and my mother, Betty, and yes, of course, Roberta, aka Mama Nude. Uncle Lonnie is ten years older than I am and keeps on getting Joyce and me in trouble. One day it was so sunny and hot in Brooklyn, and we wanted to go to the swimming pool, of course, we could not swim. Lonnie said, "Betty said it is okay for you all to go to the pool." So, we walked to Prospect Park, and somewhere in the area was a pool, it seems like it was across the street from the park. So many kids were there sitting alongside the pool, splashing in the water laughing, talking, and having fun. At five and six years old, we got to explore a lot on our own; these are the wow moments. Joyce and I stood outside the high black iron fence looking in at the kids having fun, wishing we could go inside and just put our toes in the water. We stood outside until it was almost dark and then decided to walk back home. Once we hit our block and saw the stoop, there was our mother, Betty. She was furious, could see it in her face. When she got us behind closed doors, we got the country whipping;

you know the talking with every hit. "I thought someone had taken, and you'll think something bad had happened. I was worried, don't ever do that again. Out of breath, yelling still, "Get to bed right now." Got me all worried, searching everywhere and nowhere to be found. Joyce and I wondered why she beat us if she was so glad that we are back and safe. For years we could not understand that rational. My mother was not the one to punish us. It was always the wicked Nude. But this time, the lesson needed to stick, and the beating remembered. Therefore, it was best for the one that doesn't punish to deliver the punishment. Yes, I remember it 49 years later, and that was the first and last time my mother gave me a whipping or any form of punishment. I was a good girl from that day forward; I practiced learning by other's examples. If Joyce did something wrong, I was not following suit, and she got that beating alone. Lonnie, the throne in my side, would ask me to pick his musty toe jam big toe for a nickel. Of course, I did because I like my Twinkies, popsicles, and slices of cheese pizza. I would lie for him when he was hiding on top of the roof so the school officials would not find him. Lonnie and Prince look like twins, but Lonnie was a little taller, today there is no comparison. He is more like the super from the project cartoon. Crack can mess up a face. Lonnie taught me how to tie my shoes, dance while standing on top of his feet, and how to suck his dick before I was seven years old. Uncle Junior was the best as kids say today, he remembered every Birthday, he bought us doll babies, boxes of pretty suits and dresses, and it was as if every day was Easter. But you still had to suck Uncle Lonnie dick. Uncle Junior was the best dancer, cut the scissors, the jerk, tap dancing, and so forth, he taught me. He and my father Billy were good friends; he kept up with his whereabouts for many years. My uncle Junior love older women; he was so smooth. I watched him operate one woman in the living room. They kissed and hugged and mashed against each other bodies and made funny noises while standing up. I decided at that moment that I was never going to do that. It is too nasty; he put his tongue in her mouth, and they were sucking and sucking. He moved on to the next woman in the side bedroom next to the street. The décor of the bedroom was appealing to the eyes, and I am sure it was good on the hips and back. Mama Nude like everything beautiful, so the bedrooms had a country feel, silk spread, and drapes to match with pleats, deep, feet sinking, throw rugs to rest your tired feet on upon rising, teal green and charcoal gray shimmering off the lamps. I watched Judy as she waited in the living room. I was curious to see what would take place next. So, in between the little rascals and Superman I sat in the kitchen and watched all three rooms. Diane was in bedroom one, and then he cunningly crossed over to Sliver in bedroom two. I don't know what went on with Diane and Sliver, but he spent a long time with both women in each room. Between his back and forth, he noticed that I was watching and would give me a wink as not to blow his cover. Eventually, all three of the women left, and my question was, why did you do that? Keep them in separate rooms. His reply was, "well, they have to be treated equally special. No one needs to know the others exist, especially in the same place. Handsome and charismatic, slim, tall 6'5", dark and well endowed, I did not suck his dick, just walked in on him. He loved music, could play any instrument by ear. Fascinating man! He informed me that there is nothing a young woman could do for him; older women had all he needed. Moving along, it is time to show the tail off my mother, Betty. Betty was a rebel, she was both country and city, and we often visit both. During the warm summers when school was out, we traveled by bus or train to South Carolina with our mother. She had a steady man for the country –Jimmy, and if he acted up, it was Shy or Woody. I saw Shy running down the hill one evening, kicking up dust, she had shot the rifle at him and not up in the air. I watched my mother, and how she handled men, she was a fighter. She could stab you, shoot you, or cut you without blinking an eye. When I was seven years old, she told me of an ordeal between her and my father, Billy. She was nine months pregnant and sent my father to the store for some ice cream. It seems like he was gone too long, so she opened the door to the apartment and looked out into the hallway. By God, he was there in the hallway, chatting it up with the building slut. Betty smiled and batted for him to come inside, unknowing she had a knife waiting behind her back. As soon as he stepped inside the apartment, she closed the door and stabbed him in the back, once, twice, three times. For weeks he was in agony and had to sleep on his knees, remembering he took too long to bring Betty her ice cream. My mother showed me how she carved 'Billy" in her left forearm with a hotwire. She was twenty-five. I witness most of her country relationships because there was really no place to go other than the Juke Joints down the street. Sometimes she and her boyfriend would go for long rides in the country and park in a graveyard and have drinks, corn liquor, scrap-iron, that shit other people cook up in the woods. My sister Joyce and I would be in the backseat way into the night. This was a scary time, oak trees and mossy tree limbs, look like a million different things as you driving down a road late at night with no street lights. There was so much moss hanging off the tree limbs swaying over the highways or tree branches on the left side of the road, meeting in the middle with the right side of the road shadows locking together, that would cause an imaginative child to have nightmares while awake. I am letting it all go starting from this point. There will be no more shame, hurt, anger, or pain. Softly, I will build a vision of my childhood that hopefully, you can see with me.

At home was a shotgun house in the beautiful Low Country of Coosawhatic, South Carolina, in the late 1960s. It was easy to maintain the average standard of living when your great-grandparent is from the generation of cotton picking. In the year of 1966, there was a lot that, as a child, I had no understanding of my extended environment. But things seemed good and effortless, we had food, it may have been fried fish, rice and fish grease sprinkled over the rice, but it was so good. We had homemade biscuits with sugar cane syrup or cornbread with Kool-Aid or sweetened water. By the strengths of my great-grandmother Locke, my sister Joyce and I were happy-hop-skipping home-made mop riding horsey children.

As a child, we were taught by Mama. We called her Mama because she raised us. My grandmother was called Mama

Nude, and my mother, we called her by her first name Betty. She was more of a big sister, spent some time with us when she came to visit from New York, braided our hair, and brought us stylish clothes from New York, City. Mama Nude was the bad one, she always wanted to whip you for whatever reason, and I just thought she did not like me much for some reason unknown to me and beyond my years of reasoning. Mama was the best of all, she instilled in Joyce and I that we should be strong women, more so strong-willed, have high morals to stand upon, because we may only have each other to lean on.

The morals that were embedded in my memory came from women of many trials and tribulations, but she was a woman of God and strong in the word. She was born in 1902 and had one sister, yet her father was one of thirteen siblings from Frampton Plantation. I love the stories she told about her days as a child and an adult. She had some hard times and sad times but never frond on her experiences. God was her co-pilot and never steered her wrong. I can recall her telling me of the detrimental period she faced during the Depression. She did not have shoes to put on her feet while working in the fields on Frampton Plantation, and they lived off the land. Her shoes were so worn and torn she had to put pieces of a cardboard box as the sole of her shoes. This kept her feet from being completely wet and touching the ground. Mama Locke wore shoes of this condition for years while working in the fields, yet the worst was during the Depression when they were given stamps to buy items such as food and clothing, but shoes had to wait a while.

Out of habit, she found this to be comfortable and would never throw away a pair of worn-out shoes. She used them as slippers. Her unchanged ways of simplicity brought tears to my eyes that ran down my cheeks. I try to hide my tears by turning my head and wiping my eyes quickly. Yet, returning attentively to engage in her beautiful story that I can see as she spoke each word. This left me so filled with sadness from her experience, as I glanced down at her feet, and the worn slippers. Her shoes were old brown penny loafers that she had walked on the back of and cut out a hole on the side of each big-toe for her bunion to stick out.

Mama Locke often told us of how Mama Nude worked at her side as a little girl, sweating in the hot sun. Mama Nude was eager to please her mother because she knew she still had work to do at home. Mama Locke cooked the meals, and Nude cleaned the kitchen afterward. Although she was of short stature at the time, she stood on the washtub to be tall enough to reach the sink. Mama Nude was thin, with dark chocolate velvety skin with high cheekbones, a gift that her Indian grandfather and a smile to brighten the dimmest day. Nude stood tall enough on a tin washtub to do the dishes after dinner. She was respectful of her mother, sure not to grunt or moan if she did not want to do the dishes out of share fair of the possible punishment, a backhand slap. During this time, a glance from your parents was enough; not many words needed to be used.

Nude was aware of how hard it was for her mother, so doing her part made her and her mother happy. Mama

Locke was on her second husband, and Nude did not really care for her stepfather, he was too strict. Women in the family did not stay with the men for long periods, rather it was death or divorce, and they were gone for one of these reasons. Years passed; Nude got married to a man she thought was her age. In the beginning, when they started the courtship, AC and Nude were the same height. Nude, however, continued to grow three to four inches above AC. She rendered him to be a little old man that fooled her into marriage because he did not grow any taller.

Nude endured her marriage that produced three children; Betty in 1941, Jocephus in 1942, and Lonnie in 1949. Another one to flee, Nude left AC in Savannah, Georgia, in 1949 and went to Brooklyn, New York, pregnant with Lonnie. Upon arriving in Brooklyn, Nude was alone and on her own. She found domestic work with a family that liked her and how she worked. Nude was really a beauty, with charm, charisma, and much attitude after running away from her womanizing husband, AC. Nude was presented with many different options that would afford her and her children a better life. She was offered a part in a movie, but Mama Locke advised her against the troubles that could arise from doing such type of work.

Ten to twenty years passed, and she continued to do domesticated work, taking care of other people's families and thinking about what life would have been like if she had followed her heart. Nude had no problems bringing up her children or providing for them. Hard work was okay because she came from the fields of cotton picking.

The lessons of her mother and her life had gotten her through the hard knots. This was an art form, and she applied this to the teaching of her children, hoping and praying they would pass it on. Locke was a God grateful old woman, now an asthmatic with COPD, yet, still in control and filled with wit and southern charm. She smoked a pipe, dipped snuff, chewed apple sun-cured tobacco most of her life. When her pipe was broken, she would roll a few Prince Albert's. I especially hated emptying her spit cans and cleaning her pipes.

The pipes were the worst, a six-year-old could imagine tasting, and at least it was for me. To make sure the pipe stem was clear, you had to blow it out or draw it in, and at times, that nasty black wet old tobacco came into your mouth. That taste was worse than any homemade de-worming medicine she gave, every. I sat in silence and admired her in her rocking chair, thinking how the years were starting to take a toll on her body; working in the wet fields was not good for her bones. I imagine I would not have survived those days she had lived. She told stories of walking for long hours in the hot sun on her way home that caused the bunions on her feet. When the bunions (corns) got really hard, they were more painful, and she would shave them down with a razor blade, like chipping fatwood from an old tree. It was heartfelt listening to her tell us how sometimes her shoes were too small, and this made the bunions worse. Mama Locke, shoe size was a twelve, and she was more than six feet tall with long gray plats, one on each side of her face, hanging loosely on her chest.

Getting up in years and health failing, Nude invited her mother to New York for a chance to see if her health would improve. The city seemed to make her condition worsen; it was harder for her to breathe. After seeing a doctor, she was sent back to the South for good clean oxygenated air from the towering green trees.

Upon Locke's arrival, Betty had already moved out, and only Junior and Lonnie remained in the home, which also included Joyce and me during the summer. The two of us could pass for identical twins dressed in plaid skirts with a split and a large pin on the side and a white blouse that button up from the front. We wore lace socks and black patent leather shoes with a strap that fasten on the sides. Our hair was pressed and parted down the middle of or head in two cornrows that were tied together with a white ribbon, and we sported wide bangs that hang on our forehead.

We as children loved our great-grandmother, but even more, loved the idea of her cooking each of us our personal sweet potato pie. The eldest child got the dishpan, and the youngest got the big long silver spoon. This dishpan could hold enough sweet potatoes to make 20 pies and last only until tomorrow. I was always over joyous to see her, I knew she would spend every moment she could with me telling stories about her upbringing, showing pictures of her travels and friends some here and some gone. Mama Locke started a new quilt with Joyce and me; however, it usually took a few visits before it was completed. She was so good at doing handcrafts; she could make something out of nothing. The quilts were so heavy, and once you were under it, there was no moving. There was something about her spirit, she just knew things and said things that came to be.

My mother, Betty, was working as a housekeeper and part-time waitress to have enough to make ends meet. However, her income was still at the poverty level. Therefore, she sorts out other resources, such as welfare and child support. It was her choice at this point in her life not to continue a relationship with her children's father. It was obvious to her that his life was headed down the road to no return. Betty had two beautiful Angels; Joyce and Shasha. She frequently explained to them that all they have is God and each other as a family, and they had to help support each other physically and emotionally throughout life. Mama Locke's arrival was a rescue for Betty, as she was willing to take Joyce and me with her back to Pocotaligo, South Carolina.

Betty's life improved, she went to a trade school and made education a priority. She was the first to graduate from high school in her family and obtain a certification. Since Betty was determined to better her status, she applied and was accepted to Brooklyn Community College as a full-time student. She continued to work at old odd end jobs to cover her expenses and help support her girls. Her mother, Nude, and Grandmother Locke took care of the girls because family always took care of family. If there were only two spoonful's left to eat, Joyce got one, and I got the other, and she prayed for the same or a little more for tomorrow. Mama Locke was able to take care of us, but she fell and had broken a few ribs. Something spooked the horse and threw her out of the wagon, hunting squirrels and rabbits can be dangerous.

Betty came to South Carolina to help Mama Locke until she was up on her feet again. This took some time, and healing was slow and painful for Mama Locke. Betty decided to look for work because in the evenings, Joyce and I could take care of Mama. We gave her the medicine just like Dr. Mays told us, and to make sure she did not move too much. She often told us we would make good nurses one day.

By word of mouth, Betty learned of a government program called Manpower. This program assisted those in need and wanted to return to school. The program covered the cost, transportation to and from, college tuition and a $50.00 stipend if you maintained a 100% attendance rate and a 2.0 GPA. Indeed, this was a great opportunity, and Betty surely took advantage of this blessing. Locke and Nude were so proud of Betty and her endeavors.

Betty was the first of three generations to receive a higher degree. She reached her milestone in 1970 after graduating from Talladega College in Alabama and Tuskegee in 1974 with a Master's Degree in Bio-Chemistry.
All the family members were present for this grand event, Betty's graduation. This was her special day in three ways. Firstly, she was the first to get past a 5th-grade education in

all three generations. Secondly, she had accomplished a goal that her mother and grandmother had prayed for again and again for many years. Betty was now in a place that was good and unfamiliar, and she was sure this was divine guidance because it was a rough road.

Life lessons often threw stones, and Betty was facing a devastating surgery related to cervical cancer. Betty was aware of this diagnosis a few weeks before her college graduation. She postponed the surgery until after graduation; she was trying not to be depressed during one of her brightest moments in life. Four weeks thereafter, Betty went under the knife. However, the Physician was able to complete the surgery as an outpatient. Same-day surgery was not what she thought; it turned out awfully painful for a few days. The procedure was successful, and her recovery speedy.

In the following six months, Locke's asthma attacks came more frequently, so her Physician advised her always to have someone at home that can help her when she had an attack. He advised her not to travel to the city often as the air is not suitable for her condition, and her breathing will improve. Betty thought of her mother Nude, being alone, but with little hesitance, she decided to move to South Carolina with Locke permanently. Her brothers could help with their mother if the need arose. She was getting tired of the back and forth between South Carolina and New York City and the daily hustle and bustle.

During the fall of 1965, my great-grandmother Locke picked my sister Joyce and I up in Brooklyn and moved us to Pocotaligo, South Carolina. Moving from Brooklyn to the South was a long ride on Amtrak, but our shoebox lunches were good. The fried chicken, homemade mustard potato salad, and sweet potato pie, in my own box was so delicious. Mama (Locke), as we always called her, had 12 acres of land in the middle of nowhere, which ended up being Interstate 95 coming through her back door. As far as my eyes could see, there were trees and tall grass. Sitting in the middle of this wilderness was a small wood cabin-like house, not much to the eyes. Seemingly resembles a slave quarter or hut, but the master house was more long-standing, and this was her own.

From across the way, I could see the roof of sliver tin that gleamed in the sunlight. There were two single windows in the font and one on the left side. Before entering the house, a narrow porch with dark brown boards nailed together that squeaked with each step you took. You could play a musical tone if you moved in a rhyme like motion. As I approached the front door, I could see royal blue wooden walls with small cracks, and you could peep through, into the next room. The ceiling was of white unpainted sheetrock. A long cast iron heater sat in the living room joined to the fireplace by a chimney pipe.

As the evening got older, Mama settled down, cleaned a little, and gathered what she needed to prepare our dinner. She built a fire in the stove; that old cast iron heater could put out some heat. Mama took the room across from the heater and gave Joyce and me the room next to hers. My sister and I jostled as we followed in our Granny's steps throughout the whole house. We had an aversion for this timorous place. It was dramatically different from the way we were accustomed to living in Brooklyn. The only source of running water was on the old rusty pump on the back porch. No inside plumbing, but a little hut a few yards from the back steps was presented to us as the "outhouse." All bodily functions took place here, the place of evacuating your intestinal contents. The slop jar was an interesting part of the bedroom décor, and it was only to be used at night when it was too dark to see if you were about to sit on a snake. My God! Emptying the slop jar that was used for those after hour's bodily functions was horrific; the stench would knock a dead man out. But you buried the contents in a hole that you turned over with a shovel or hoe, washed it out with water from the pump, and some moss. Please, never leave moss stems in the pot, it is not clean.

I was not about to enter into this hell hole with snakes crossing the seat, spiders, and bugs. I dug a deep hole in the back yard and buried whatever was in the slop jar, and that was it. Of course, nothing can prepare you for the times when your little butt would slide down into the slop jar because you forgot to hold on to the sides. Believe me, it takes two or three people to pull you out of that suction pot. Then there is the bath at the pump that followed, no hose or warm water, just splashes of cold pump water on your backside.

There were so many adventures living with Mama, we helped her build the chicken coop, and it was a bit larger than the outhouse. I was just not in the habit of going to the outhouse. A human being was supposed to use this hole in the ground with a wood door and three sides for covering. A strong frat could probably blow it over. If you got caught after the sun went down having to use the outhouse, you needed a Kerosene lamp, and a hoe to kill the snakes. I actually felt safer in the chicken coop; at least the snakes would have a choice of what to strike.

As a little girl, I can remember growing up in the country like it was yesterday. The most meaningful experiences I hold close to my heart are times spent with my great grandmother, her simple ways of life and warm evenings on the front porch or cold nights next to the fireplace eating sweet potato pie, and playing with the biddies'.

I recall the days living with my great grandmother as a little six-year-old girl. We lived on Wale's Hill in a small country town called Coosawhatcie in South Carolina. All the surrounding towns had Indian names, such as Yamasee. Actually, they were living in tepees next to the post office when we arrived in 1965. I often steered at the Indians dressed in their native attire, and one was sitting on a stool outside the post office. Mama would pull me gently to come along, but I just wanted to stand still and look. Living in this small town was a joyous experience as a child. You could absorb yourself in the rich greenery of trees, flowers, and the smell of fresh hoed grass. I especially like the four o'clock flowers; they were a rainbow of different colors. I was most amazed by these flowers because they would open every day at four o'clock. There was nothing like waking up to the sound of wild animals in the backyard, for example, rabbits, squirrels, deer, birds singing in the trees, and most of all, snakes that I hated. We were living in a shotgun house in the middle of a rain forest and a graveyard. The backyard was grassless, just white sand like from a beach, that towering green between your toes. Mama would hollow from the back porch at us to put our shoes back on before we got "the worms."

Our small two-bedroom shotgun house sat on this huge hill, fenced in from the wilderness. However, there was a gate to the left, which opened to a graveyard called Mooncepoo. Men wore orange or green and white vests with big dogs on the back of pick-up trucks, and they would drive into the graveyard to go deer hunting. They wore some unusual design clothing that resembles military uniforms with bright orange vests. Mama reminded me and my sister Joyce to stay on the porch, so we won't get in the way of incoming traffic. My great-grandmother's name was Elizabeth Chisholm, but she was best known as Mama Locke or Mrs. Locke to everyone else, including the insurance man, chicken back man and candy man. She was a lovely old woman in her 70's, always happy and in a cheerful mood. Mama had long salt and pepper hair braided in two cornrows that hung down her back. She would tie a scarf on her head and an apron around her waist. Mama did not believe in throwing anything away, so her apron was made from old clothes we had outgrown over the years.

Mama worked in the cotton fields as a child next to her parents. She often told us stories of her childhood that were sad. So, as she slipped her size 12 feet into a pair of old slides that she had cut the toes out of, I had a visual glimpse of what those days must have been like for mama. She wore simple clothes, a floral blouse, and starched (i.e., skimmed off the top of a pot of boiling rice) pleated skirts with stockings rolled up just above her knees and twisted in a knot, just tight enough to stay up on her legs for the day.

Our day would start with feeding the chickens, getting the eggs from the hen's nest, and slopping the hogs. This was so entertaining and free, we ran after the chickens, played with the biddies, and rode the hogs. This was better than chasing the ice cream truck on the streets in Brooklyn, but it took some time to digest this wilderness. When it was time for lunch, we smelled just like the pigs/hogs and looked just as dirty. She sent us to the pump to wash off the mud and leave the dirty items on the back porch. Mama was such a good cook. She made everything from scratch. Her sweet potato pies were out of this world. She had a big dishpan that she mixed the deep orange color potatoes in with other ingredients. Mama stirred for a long time as Joyce, and I watched.

Finally, she was finished, I got the pan, and Joyce got the spoon. But what we were really waiting for was the half pie she made for each of us. The crust was so good; she rolled it out with a jelly jar and cut it with the pie pan. I often wondered what made the pie so good, as I watch her roll the pieces of dough off her fingers.

Mama grew all her vegetables on her land, peanuts, collard greens, sweet potatoes, tomatoes, okra, beans, and watermelon. She digs the holes, I dropped the seeds, and Joyce would close the holes and add the water. I was the seed dropper because I was tall; therefore, the plant would reach the top of the soil faster. Mama had a reason for everything, and we believed everything she said.

Once, she told us to sit on the porch and look for the man in the moon. She gave us a slice of cold watermelon from the icebox. It was a warm evening, not much wind was blowing, and we had only church hand fans. The melon was like a drink, a thirst-quenching cold drink after running from a dog. We sat on the corner of the porch with our legs swinging back and forth, looking for the man in the moon. She always told me I have been rich with imagination and was filled with so much love. I soaked every word she spoke, every story she told, and all her homemade remedies. I felt so lucky to have Mama Locke as my mama.

Thank You Father

Thank you, Father, for the
Light within me
The love that Guides me
And soothes my Soul
Thank you, Father, for protecting me
Holding me, in open hands
So, I can withstand pain and suffering
That goes On and On
Thank you, Father,
For I know you are Always near
On Bending Knees
You
Hear my prayers
Thank you, Father, You Comfort me
You lift me
When I am in tears
As if Angel wings encasing me
In smothering warmth
Thank you, Father,

I Remember

I remembered, but I cannot remember what it felt like to have my innocence taken away at five years old. My trials and tribulations start here, carrying me from crawling to that last standing step. One never knows what life has in mind. However, for some intuitive reason, Shasha could sense what life had in store for her future; by the past few years. Enduring childhood incest, repeated raped by an old man, and then gang-raped by five young men all by the tender age of ten years old.

Well, hold on tight, between the ages of five and ten, all this reckless God forbidden mess happens. There was an old man named Dewy, and this particular old man Dewy assaulted her like she was his mail-ordered child bride. He had a dusty gray ash completion, white thick cottony hair, dressed in suits from the 1930s, and reaped of alcohol. He looked like the average drunk on the streets in Brooklyn, staggering, falling over into the sand, and crawling. Sometimes he would crawl up the hill coming to my great grandmother's house. I often prayed for him to die before he got up the hill, somehow, I knew what was next in line…me.

He was about five feet and eight inches tall with bow legs, another cousin. He imposed his sickness on a child, me. His first sneaky opportunity came when he was too drunk to go home, and my great grandmother allowed him to sleep in the same room with Joyce and me. There was an extra roll out bed in our room under the clothesline. She told him he could rest there until he was sober enough to walk home on his own accords. Please, believe this when I say life went on as usual, little did I know or understand that something was really, really wrong here. The unspeakable things that were happening to me were amiss, yes.

I was having pain in my legs to the point that on some days I could not walk. I stayed in bed, and my great grandmother would put hot towels and rub old meat grease on my legs. My stomach was always hurting, my hair was falling out, I had no appetite, and the Physician could find nothing wrong. I believed nothing was wrong like the Physician suggested. Yet, I wore my coat all day in school, and it could be 90 degrees outside. I sat in class and pulled my hair out until the top was ball...mostly because it felt good.

At My Crossroads

I give myself power today in knowing I am not alone
I stand at my crossroad looking behind
I intend to let go of despair
And find hope
Sorrow is not mine
I choose to make peace with the loss
To keep from falling apart
I will express mourning in order to move forward

I will release the rut of regret and the fear of tomorrow
At my crossroads, I will stand in God's Grace
To make way for forgiveness, pleasures, beauty, and hope
I will be empowered by my conscience, and my gift is forgiveness
I am not alone all my pain is gone

As time passed, I would play as usual with my sister Joyce. We loved to play make-believe, house, cooking, dressed up in Mama's clothes and shoes. I was the mother, and she was the baby, I would dress her up, give her a bottle, and cook dinner. I made a fire in the back yard between two bricks, with dried brown grass from the sunshine and small sticks. I placed a piece of tin over the bricks to make my stove, and the smoke started to blow, the fire was on its way. I gathered the weed that resembled collard greens, down to the smell, and boiled it in a can. Meanwhile, I was waiting for the mud pies to dry in the sun. I played with bugs, catching bright, colorful butterflies, putting lightning bugs on a string, chasing grasshoppers and lizards. I was always busy outside at home, amazed by insects and animals and the noise they made. Mama raised chickens and pigs, but they were also our constant source of entertainment and friends, it was hard to eat one for dinner, so I usually shun away from the meat.

Maybe I was not supposed to be aware of the things that were happening to me. I thank God that I was not aware of the horror in my little life. But I always prayed, I seldom pronounced the words correctly, but I prayed with my great-grand mama and sister. I prayed hard for God to take care of all those that hurt me. I watched to see if my prayers were being answered. I watched, and I watched, and I watched. I continued to have health problems, and the Physician told her I was not eating enough and not striving. Once again, my great-grandmother left the physician's office, puzzled at him telling her things will change for the better as I grew up…hum.

Today I am Grateful

That my soul rises
To set on my bedside
For my feet to hit the floor
I know
I am still alive
Today I am grateful

Yet on some nights
I rest on my back
Staring at the sky
My body feeling light
As a floating star
Feels like in this shell
I rested well
Today
I am grateful
For a lot in life

No sensation about me
My eyes the only thing
To move freely
I see the
Beginning of a new day
In endless time
I am grateful
The Lord kept me in mind

Mama tried some more of her Indian home remedies, nothing improved and she began to worry. She could not understand how two children in the same house could be developing so different in every sense. Joyce was healthy, plump, and happier than I. She was so plump that her nickname was Pig. Shasha always felt she was the outsider, not related to the family; she was different and was treated differently, the black sheep. She looked different, acted differently, and behaved differently. Joyce, on the other hand, was picture-perfect, eye full of beauty, and praised in front of Shasha for her good looks. Shasha builds up some bad feelings or just outright raging dislike for these individuals.

Dr. Mays, our family Physician, often made house calls, came around more often, not sure why. Maybe he was trying to figure out or see what was going on with me. He was a nice older white man that seemed extremely nice to us. He told us how to take care of mama when she had an asthma attack. As a child, I started to like his visits, and I felt safer. He was always concerned about my leg pain, and all I could do was stay in bed and keep warm towels on my legs for a few days. Eventually, the pain would subside, and I could stand and walk again. There were so many things going on with my body, and I suppose it started on my mind next.

I Found Me

Not knowing I was lost
Locked inside myself
Unable to see
The things that might be
Able to set me free

I Found Me

Silently waiting alone
For what
Only if I had known
In the darkness
I roam for the
 Spirit to touch me
Let me know
 I am not alone

I Found Me

I could see three shadows in the wire clothesline over there
in the corner close to the entrance into the kitchen (i.e.,
keep in mind we were living next to a large Graveyard).
Two were men and one was a woman, and she stood in the
middle. Sometimes they were at the foot of the bed or on

the side next to me (i.e., dark shadows). I was not afraid until one night while in bed with the lights off, it felt like one of them had hit me in the head. I could see the shadows beside my bed; I always slept in the front and Joyce in the back. At this point, I covered my head and became very afraid of the dark. The hit was so hard, and I was so afraid under my great grandmother's homemade quilt; I wept and lay still until I did not know I was asleep. Neither my sister nor my mama ever knew this took place I kept it locked inside with everything else. Now, in addition to wearing my coat all year round, I now sleep with my head covered up no matter how hot it was or in any season.

The rooster would crow early in the morning as the sun rises, another day before me with uncertainty. Mama asks us to go hunting with her for squirrels and rabbits. Maybe we can hunt down our dinner for tonight, and she smiled, I sure did not feel like chasing any headless chicken. This was a good start for mama, no asthma last night, so she rested well. She trusted us enough to give us rifles, and the hunting took place behind the house in the Graveyard. I should have used this on old man Dewy, but I did not have the heart to even step on a worm, we did not have roaches. Guess our living quarters were already too much like outdoors for the roaches. It was a wild kingdom basically up to our back porch. Almost every animal you could imagine in a swamp, again, there were deer's, rabbits, squirrels, snakes, turtles, birds, and so on. It was always something there for me to keep my mind and attention on.

Depending on what we were having for dinner, Joyce and I always cleaned the meat. I never killed any animals big or small nor ate squirrels and rabbits. I really did not care much for the cleaning, and after the cleaning, I really did not like the way they looked back at me, so I ate nothing related to that sort of meat. On the road going back home, we stopped to pick up fatwood. This helps the fire to burn without using too much kerosene in the old wood heater and stove. We picked a few pieces of oak wood hanging loosely from a tree, and a couple of dry sticks, all to make the fire catch easier. After building the fire, we settled around the stove to parch pecans, peanuts, and roast sweet potatoes in the ashes. Mama did so many things that were simple with us and enjoyable for all.

I love the smell of nature in the swamp, climbing the trees, and gathering moss. Moss was a necessity, our toilet tissue. There was an art to wiping your rear end with this part of nature. If you did it incorrectly, you were left pulling out the little moss stubs, and that is not a nice chore. I could smell the rain in the air before the first drop fell on the tin roof of our shot-gun house so refreshing. I would stand in the front yard; hold my head back, catching the drops as they fell from the sky.

Minutes or days would pass, and all the beautiful things in the world that surrounded me were shaken up by Dewy. When he came to visit and stayed the night, that gloomy cloud was over my head once again. As a child, good things went as fast as they came, but the bad lingered for a while in a corner, and I ignored it. After he was gone, good things were renewed again as if the rain went away and the sun shines again, and the shadows parted. After this visit and Dewy was gone, Mama, Joyce, and I started on a new quilt. We loved to sew by hand; Joyce and I would cut out the patches from old clothing that we no longer were using. It was important to make sure that all were the same size. We made double lining quilts, which were so heavy you only needed one for the whole winter. Mama always worked on the lining alone, but we watched and threaded the needles. Her eyesight was too bad to see the small hole of the needle eye.

When we took breaks from quilting, it was to the kitchen for homemade sweet-potatoes pies, and it was never enough. I would roll out the pie crust, and Joyce helped with stirring the potatoes. She showed me how to use a Ballard glass jar to roll out the pie crust and carefully place it in the oiled pan. Some pies had a top crust, and others were folded over and pinch around the edges. Mama grew her vegetables in the field behind the chicken coup and next to the outhouse, between two sets of manure. She said that the sun shined brighter on this side of the house. Since I was the tallest, I got to drop the seed and Joyce would close the holes up and pour the water on top of the soil. Mama explained that the sprout would be tall or come faster if the tallest one of us dropped the seed. We did have nice long sweet potatoes for our pies and chips.

When mama made a pie, Joyce got the pan, and I got the spoon. Next time, I got the pan, and Joyce got the spoon. She tried to keep things equal. She made each of us a half pie to have all by ourselves. Our best times were spent doing things together. Mama liked to take us fishing and crabbing down the railroad tracks or under the bridges in

Coosawhatchie, and it was so noisy when the train passed. We waved hurriedly at the passengers on the train, not knowing if they saw us or not. Mama would yell, get ya'll asses from up there before you fall and your mama kill me. Crabbing was my favorite. No bait required (i.e., worms), just neck-bone tied at the end of some box string (part of a tree branch with a thick string wined around it), and a dipping net. If the tide was coming in it was good for the crabs because they would be close to the water's edge. We spent most of the time under the railway of the bridges; there we could go in the shade when it was too hot. Mama was a woman that lived off the land.

Reflecting back, things appear to have started badly at a young age and continued. The hardest test, as I picture this, is being raped. Pinned down and pressed upon by relatives that thought a ten- year old should have a boyfriend and taught a valuable lesson. I was petrified as I was forced on my back for hours as they took turns running this 'TRAIN." As these animals did this horrific, brutal act, I prayed in silence for this to end. I felt nothing; I coiled inside myself as tears rolled down my high round cheeks. It seems as they explained, "other girls your age were willing, and enjoying being "broken–in" this was the experience. You cannot say you are not interested and get away with it, "no way."
What went through my mind was that I would have to see these same boy's day after day. They went to the same school, rode the same school bus, stood at the same bus stop, and one was the actual bus driver. Now, to leave the city seemed trivial too, coming to the country and facing such harsh violations on a child, as young as I. My mother

wanted to escape the dangers and horror of Brooklyn, New York, and landed me in a snake nest.

Imagine

Alone to imagine her real anguish
Frozen deep, seeping to the top
Yet not beneath
Boundless emotions disrupt

A phantom lover's heart
Becomes widowed and sets in solitude
Holding on
 To be a desire
Which no rare love will flee
Such fire burning
 Inside me

Alone to image her real anguish
Torn between hollow tress
Ceaseless emotions erupt
Trickles into the lover's heart
 As she bends to her knees
Awakens
 A thieving love
Deeply given to the child
That could only
Imagine

Trying My Best

At home in the Low Country of Beaufort, South Carolina, trying to make ends meet is rather tough. Morals take the better part of you and food on the table and paying the bills takes precedence over all other things. So, one night, my uncle asked me to give a package to one of his friends that was going to stop by, I know what is in the bag, and I believe it isn't doing much harm to sell a nickel bag of weed here and there. A little voice would say that it is wrong; "you're helping other people children get into drug abuse."

Shasha could not see herself harming someone else or their children for a dollar.
The kids at school knew her uncle and that he was a dealer. They would ask her to bring a few bags to the school. However, she refused, realizing the risk was not worth it. Hustling was not in her makeup; besides she was terrified of jail, from the stories alone.

Shasha's family was into the business, uncle, grandmother, great grand auntie, and many cousins. They stood to the head of the road stopping the cars before they could enter the subdivision of Green Acres. The entire drug situation started with Uncle Junior in the 1970s when he ran away from those chasing him, whether in actuality or in his mind. He left Brooklyn, New York, in a hurry to end up in Ridgeland, South Carolina, with his only daughter at the time. His presence changed the entire neighborhood, from the eldest person to the youngest. No one in the neighborhood knew of anything other than whiskey, and now he brings the devil to the front door, drugs...well weed mostly.

All the family members lived in the same subdivision of Green Acres. Great-grandmother Locke lived on the left side of the road about the 10th house. Nude live in the 5th house on the right side of the road, Betty his sister lived in the 3rd house on the back street. Locke's evil and jealous sister Rebecca and her family live 3 houses further down the street from Locke's home. There were two wars going on here, a war of drugs and getting ahead of the Jones's. These are my school days from the 7th grade to the 12th grade. I was very studious, and I came home from school, did my homework. I went outside and played baseball with my friends in the neighborhood or basketball. I was 5'9" and a size zero, size nine in shoes, tall and slim, beautiful, flawless bronze skin tone with short wooly-curly hair in an afro, in the 7th grade, and maybe 90 pounds. My lips were full, and my eyes were brown, which seems to lighten in the sunshine. I was flat chest with a round shapely butt, much like my mother. If I was a boy, I would have been really handsome, or so they told me. One day I hope to be.

A Woman

Dazzling with courage
Daring in love
Eloquent with her emotions
Suave with her grace

A woman
Is the quintessence
A man yearns for
A woman gracious and merciful
In giving genuine love
Has he found it?
From her deepest core
Love
That knows no bounds
A Woman

That is what I experienced.

Larry

Now my favorite type of man is the married ones, "just kidding." For instance, there are a few that have passed through my timely years at some point. To start, I will speak of Mr. Bending my knees, tall, handsome, spitting image of Denzel Washington, 20 years ago. Still looking delicious today-he stood at six feet and nine inches, 210lbs.-muscular, with a low fade like a bronze goddess. Beautiful man, I love his walk, he glides in confidence. I met Mr. Bending Knees in South Carolina in the summer of 1995. I did not ask any questions, just having fun and enjoying life, a free spirit. I would drive from Atlanta to see him for a few hours or a few days, however long it took us to get over the craving for each other.

After six months, this mother fucker told me he was married. My heartfelt as if it had been stricken by lightning. I was so into this man and the passion we shared I just could not stop seeing him, nope could not do it. I have never smoked, drank, or use drugs, yet, I was addicted to Mr. Bending Knees; he was my crack. He was five years older than I, and he was concerned about my intimate experience along the line of satisfaction.

I like this about him because he was going to deliver what I missed out on.
You see, I had my first orgasm at the tender age of 35, yes unbelievable-right? I was in LOVE, you hear me. I am still at awe-35. I enjoyed and looked forward to the Fridays when he would soon arrive. I would greet him at the door,

with nothing on most of the time, not all the time. Basically, he never saw me with clothes on, or maybe once for a few minutes until we got in the car. The car was parked on the side of my apartment building, Snap-finger Crest, in Decatur, Georgia. We got in the back seat of his Range Rover and layout, sprawling naked. All I had to do was flip that dress over my head, and it was on. His lips touched mine so tenderly, and as he gently slid his tongue into me, then our lips pressing more firmly as he held me tight in his rock iron arms. My body heated from head to toe. I could hardly stand for him to touch me. My body shook and quivered as we embraced our warm moist bodies as one. Larry caressed and maneuvered his hands all over my body, touching two and three hotspots at a time.

We would spend so much time together. Even the twenty minutes stop between going to the store and returning to his home was enough for that moment. He only lived about five minutes away from my apartment, so convenient, right? This relationship continues for three years. Sad for me, a friend that I treated like a sister came between us, and it was over. That Whitney Houston wannabe butt forehead bitch decided it was no big deal. What could I say or do, nothing, but called his wife- you can imagine the rest, I will not let you one up me cocksucker? I call her boyfriend Jayme (older, married, marine, and from Panama). "Hey man got a word for you, your girl has about 15 credit cards in your name, and she is now fronting as your wife. She is also fucking, Paul, David, and Bobby from Paris Island and Jimmy, Robert, and Joe from the Air station. I just thought you needed to know that bit of information. I called her and told her, "thank you for opening my eyes, stink bitch. I thought you were a friend, but you only used me to get to what was not mine as well. When you punched holes in my dining room chair with the nail file, I looked at you and did not call you on it. It was unbelievable, but when kissed and fondled him, you did this in front of my brother and daughter, you let the dragon out bitch. I am going to let all your dicks know you are the dripping asshole they know you to be." Fifteen years later, I see him in a restaurant. I am happy like a little girl in a candy shop.

As we pass each other, I call him, and he calls out to me, and here comes the embrace. Oooh, to be in his arms standing straight, felt like I had tasted the best chocolate that melts so velvety in your mouth. I am not one for holding grudges… He smelled so good; his body was still firm, muscular, and lean. Flirting as I do, I asked if he was going to be my Christmas present, we exchange numbers, and he said: "is tomorrow too soon?" I smiled and left the building. Tomorrow was not too soon.

We met up that Friday evening at about 7pm. I went home, took a nice bubble bath, soaked my special areas, and made my toes suckable. I met him at his office, drove up, and park my car in the visitor space. He walked over, body so erected like he has a slow march going on, opened the car door, and took me by the hand. I was thinking, *lead me on to ecstasy*-as, we walked into his office. We passed a wide-open area of the office. I thought he was going to take me at that moment, wishful thinking; my "money" was pulsating. We entered his office, secluded from what seemed like the world. I sat in the empty chair facing his desk as he stared over at me. He took the Captain's seat. We smiled and kept repeating each other's name, "Larry," I said, "Shasha," he replied, "oh, Larry," I said. "Oh, Shasha," he said, and his lips were on mine.

 He kisses me as I sat in the chair and raised my head so our lips would not part. Suddenly my dress was on the floor, and my heels were all I was left wearing. I was wearing a sexy align tan button up the front linen dress, easy access, no need to be wrapped up in all that cloth. Besides, he never really saw me in clothes much before now. He made this delicious noise, "hum mm" and "dammm," followed. We lay on the floor on the floor in front of the Captain's chair, and he had his way with me as if we had never been apart for so many years. He gently kisses my lips, neck, and my left nipple, that is the sensitive one. He rests one hand on my neck as he kissed further down my waist to my top hat. At heaven's door, he stopped, my legs trembled the closer he got-while anticipating the slide-in of his moist lips and warm tongue. His tongue could rest on his chin, and a peak tipped out, hard.

He was my clit-sucker, and he is back, just for a moment. I was so hot, sweating, and panting trying, trying and trying not to let loose. Uncontrollable, shaking I had no control at the mere touch of his hands. He caressed my clit with his lips and carefully sucked away. He came up, and our lips met again, I never disliked this part, shit I tasted pretty good. I turned my head and climbed into the Captain's chair. There I knelt at ease the letdown was coming as he closed in on the Money. For a few minutes, it was hard to penetrate, but there was pleasure in this pain. In passion, I called out his name over and over and over. He moves faster, harder, deeper, asking, "Baby is it too much?" "Oh, oh, no, no, it is so good, it has been so long, don't stop, please don't."

We changed positions, each better than the last. He led me to the conference room and positioned me on the table. The moonlight was shining in on us, enjoying the show as well. He put my legs over his broad shoulders and pulled my hips closer into his, into his...for an hour non-stop, I backed away, I pushed him away, and the "Money" was running.

I was so taken; I took it out and pressed my mouth upon the head of this magnificent king for a brief relief. He enters the playground one more time, and the end of the night was explosive, like fireworks in Disneyland.

After a week, he called, wondering why I had not called him. I said, "I thought it was a one-time thing." He said, "hell no, an everyday thing," and laughed. I really loved this man in the past, and I knew what could happen if I continued with this recreation activity. I pondered with the thought of us all over again, and the adult in me kept saying you want a man all to yourself, no more sharing or shortchanging. Of course, I rationalized, over and over in my head why it would be good for me, shit everyone needs love, passion, and pleasure.

He lives so close by; he is exactly what I desire. He knows me, my body, and my thrills. I even wondered if this was a test from God to see if I had matured over the years. So, I prayed that if this man is not meant to be in my life, let him be gone. Take the thoughts of him out of my mind, but they got stronger, like hunger. Day in and day out, he was on my mind.

Every day I thought of him and me together as lovers. I longed so much for someone to touch me in the right way to feel the right things in the right places.

Weeks passed, and I did not call him, nor did he call me. After about two months, I made reservations at the Marriott for four days to get away from the family. I stayed in the room every day, looking at his number, in between sleep and homework. Should I or should I not. Actually, during my stay, I had a choice of three adoring men, but I really wanted just the one and was actually afraid of the other two. So, juggling the idea of who would keep me company and *enjoy* all the Hotel/amenities the room had to offer, which included all of me.

My dear longtime friend John was number one on my list because I knew he was afraid as well and would not come, no matter how much he wanted to have me. I have known John for 18 years and attracted to him just as long. Seventeen years passed before he let me known that the feelings were mutual but we only remained friends. During this time, we hugged once, playfully displaying our

emotions on his Birthday. He is married, but was single when I first met him; I guess this was a missed opportunity according to him. So, I did not call him. The other gentlemen, you could not even guess what he is about.
Therefore, I will enlighten you. He is a Pastor. I call him the titty man. He loves breasts; they are such a turn on for him. Ok, he came over for some titty action for a few minutes. I do have a strong attraction for him, but he too is a married man. I run from him because I know where it may lead. I don't want to be in that flesh situation with a Pastor.

So, I am in the room alone, finishing up an assignment online for school. I dialed Larry's number and hung up before he answers. He calls back, "Did you call me"? "Yes, I did, would you like to come over this morning and play for a few hours?" I could hear the joy in his voice from the first word he spoke, but only a few hours." He asked, "Where are you?" I replied, "Marriot, off of 20 West, just before the Airport. I am on the 14th floor in room 1404, and the door will be open. He said I am already on 20 and can be there in 10 minutes. I was standing next to the window wrapped in a short towel with my hair hanging down my back, just like he like it. He walks up to me and pulls the towel down, "baby, you smell so sweet, can I taste you?" I replied, "Since when do you ask?"
He rests his clothes on the chair, picks me up, and lay me gently in the bed. The curtains are closed; the TV is off and love songs playing in my head. He whispered in my ears, "Baby, please don't keep me waiting so long. We are going

to have to do something about this torture," as he climbs on board.

TOO Short Paul

In the past 2 years, I have met men from 4'8" to 5'3",
dressed like professors in blue checkered suits with bow
ties or casual and too laid back. "In the club," I was
wondering who let this child in here in his Easter suit. To
my surprise, he was bold enough to come over and ask me
for a dance. Okay, I am 5'9" and wore 2" heels, so I smiled
and politely said, "Yes." He was so confident, as we dance,
and I compared his height to my 8-year-old grandson, and
my grandson was taller. "So, what is your name," he asks, I
replied, "Shasha and yours, Dr. Goke." He led me back to
my table, and we exchanged numbers. We often spoke on
the phone, but I never went out with him on a date. I just
felt there was something irregular about this. However, to
make a long story short, I meet another sweet soul, Paul.
We had mutual friends in common that set us up on a blind
date. I was forewarned of his statue and a few other issues.
He was taller than Dr. Goke, by at least 3 inches. So, I
agreed to go to a movie with Paul on our blind date. It was
a weekday, so the movie was not going to have many
people. We met at the theatre a few blocks from my job. He
was filled with enthusiasm while describing himself to me
over the phone, this was so I could recognize him and what
he was driving, and I did the same with hesitance. When I
saw that head, it was shaped such as this ^-^ I almost drove
off but reframed from being judgmental. I was told once,
"Good things come in small packages."
Speeding along with this story, he tells me what he likes in
a woman. Mind me not, our friend has already enlightened

me on the type of women he has been dating. Yes, let's say
they are not in the image of OPRAH, but maybe in the area
of 500lbs. So, I am listening and getting fired up. He tells
me, I don't go out to movies, I don't' eat out, I don't travel
and I, I, I, can you clean? I am trying to remain calm and
polite, and I asked, "Have you ever considered a Maid?"
So, I just look at him in disbelief and turn to watch the
movie. So, we never went out on a date again. Yet, Paul
was always calling for me to come to his home. My
question here was why I would leave the comfort of my
home to go to your home to do the same thing I am doing at
home. If I went to a movie, dancing, or dinner, he would
question why he was not invited. I gracefully reminded him
that he does not do these things. We have remained distant
friends for years; he is a funny little guy. I asked him one
day, "who is taller, you or Willie?" and he said, "I am." I
asked Willie, "who is taller, you or Paul," and he replied, "I
am." In my observation, they are both 5'3". Things just
were not measuring up for me. Paul is the spitting image of
Steve Harvey, and his little chest just blows up whenever I
mention the resemblance. Paul can only have two types of
conversations, "money and flipping houses" not interested
in your money, it's your money. I can't stand a man that
flaunts his money. I maintained my dry spell and worked
on my spirituality, self- healing and education a lot of
education. I know when a change is needed.

Joe

Today is a beautiful sunny day in the city of Decatur. So, I will talk about Joe since he thinks he is a Bronze Goddess. I met Joe at the Air Station enlisted club in Beaufort, South Carolina. I noticed him about a year earlier, as he would often visit my workplace for dinner with his beautiful fiancé. He was a very attractive man, six feet–two inches tall, honey-golden completion, and smooth silky, flawless skin. His hair cut in a military fade, close on the sides, very becoming, big ass head and sexy lips…bottom larger than the top. His smile was dazzling and bright; I fantasized about touching his lips with mine. His lower lip slightly fuller than the upper and how he seductively moistens his lips made heat rush to my special spot. I hadn't learned how to talk to my pussy (money) yet, but I was aware that she reacted to the outside appearance of men. I should have looked at those moments as warnings not to indulge and stay away. But…nope.

He was wearing a pair of linen shorts with a short-sleeve shirt and sandals, simple. I was so turned on by his walk. He moved with such carefulness as if he just might crush something if he moved to fast. His legs had just a slight curve, and I often thought what a handsome man and we could do beautiful things together. I wished for him to be mine. *Damn wishes* do come true. I thought to myself as I often did, he must be very generous; she was sporting a huge diamond- at least 3 carats no less. He opened the car door for her, kept one hand on her as they walked in and out of the restaurant, and gave her a kiss before she sat in the car. Joe drove a 280 Z Fair-lady, slick and black, with the CD player on the ceiling of the car and the steering wheel on the right side of the car. He loves to listen to Sade, Muddy Waters, Kenny G, and smooth jazz. Whatever his appetite called for, rather it was partying or thinking. Joe spent a lot of time thinking... about what I have no idea. He was private about his life, especially business adventures. I was curious about the business side of his life other than the military.

Well, after a few months, I noticed she was no longer coming to the restaurant with him. Silently, I was hoping she was gone somewhere else. Got my wish, she was gone, back to Phoenix, Arizona. So, I would speak to him more often and let the other servers know that he was my customer only customer all the time. On Wednesday nights, I would go to the Image Lounge, it was the spot and Ladies Night. The Marines, Sailors, and Airmen were out in full force. Well, the only spot in town, known worldwide by military personnel as the *joint.*

Joe came religiously on Wednesday night's; this was Ladies Night, and the club was packed never mind overcrowded fire hazard-three dollars to get in, and the party was on. I sat close to the entrance, looking good and waiting to get a peek at him. He strolls in with his group of nine, men only all looking good sporting the finest cars in town. My girls Darlene, Diane, Eleanor, and Odessa, danced most of the night. I was the observer; I had a great time at the meat market and eventually went home alone.

A few months pass, and we decided to go to the Air Station Enlisted club on a Saturday night. It was a meat market of all sorts of men, ten men for every one woman, pick a few. Out of nowhere, I bumped into Joe, and my heart jumped to my mouth. Before I could open my mouth, he said, "You stepped on my shoes." I did not say a word, and he walked off. Only to return a few hours later, he has been watching me. He said, "I would like to get to know you better." Of course, I was game, so game that my rabbit was jumping, like a tiger in Winnie-the-poo. The pulsation and throbbing sensation were strong like a heartbeat.

He took me home that night, but I did not invite him to come inside. As he walked me to my door, I could feel his body on mine following my every command. Patience and will power be such a good virtue. The following day he called and came over for a short while, and later that evening, he drove us to Savannah, Georgia, for dinner on the waterfront. We shared a breathtaking evening of good foods, spirits, and company. We got acquainted, shared life experiences and childhood memories. It felt as if I had known him all my life. For the next six to eight months, we spent a lot of time together. It got to the point where I had the keys to his house and vehicle. I was the first person he saw in the morning and the beautiful face he saw when our heads rest next to each other at night.

It is amazing how women can be so jealous, devious, and sneaky. My so-called girls thought I was the most stupendous female in the group. I like my man, get away with all sorts of shit. Eleanor and Diane would say, "Girl, you are super stupid." I believe a man is going to do whatever his head tells him, and I don't mean the head with the brain. My reasons were not to deal with things I had no control over. Besides, Joe and I had already sat down and established some ground rules. First, it was called truth or consequences, which were whatever he asked me, I had to tell the truth, and if I got angry with him, I had to wash his head (brain less head) with my lips. So, it should be obvious that I did not get upset much. Overall, we shared a good relationship, I loved him, and he loved me back. I really knew how to push his buttons, and he could not figure me out- there you have it. I was so happy. Out of the "rules," he got one thing he would never forget. I was his alarm clock for nine years. He woke up every morning at 06:00 with my lips washing his head. During the night when he rolled over, I rolled. When I turned over, he turned, or I was careful not to move, so he could sleep inside my warm cushiony pussy. Some pussy has rigid which are close, and some are far, and some have none. It's like a suction cup holding the dick in place until I turn it loose. We were so close, but things do change.

So, one day, this brave hussy bitch comes strolling by with a bottle, "is Joe home?" she asked. I replied, *no.* in my silent dialog, bitch, what the fuck gives you the nerve to come to knock on this mother-fucking door asking about my man. He is off and playing a basketball game in Charleston with the military team. He should be back in a few hours, at least. Of course, I did not share this information with her. She left when I strongly emphasized that he was not home. Thirty minutes later, she comes back again, with a bottle of liquor in her hands. "Is Joseph in?" "No, he is not, and who are you?" Oh, I am a friend of Michaels, but you are asking for Joseph. Do you mind if I wait? Wait where? This was my question. Why here? With you, I am sure he won't mind.

I am so sorry, but this girl is not in the mood for company. Apparently, she had already had too much to drink and came into the house. Okay, no respect, and the bitch had to get her ass whipped. I don't know you; Michael has never mentioned you or brought you by the weekend cookouts or on the fishing trips. I had to toss that ass like it was salad all over the house, down the hallway, on the dresser, and behind the bed. Out of nowhere, Michael walks into the bedroom. We are on the dresser, and he pulls me off of her. She was half-naked with patches of hair missing. I wanted her to look bad, bitch.

I am such a nice person that I explained to her that the ass whipping she just received had nothing to do with Joe. It was all about respect. I gave her the car and house keys and went to my apartment. Never give up your shit. About two hours later, Joe comes over to Diane's house on my ten-speed Japanese racer, searching, then Eleanor's and my mother. I was hiding in Diane's bedroom, close enough to listen to him, pleading with her to find out my whereabouts. I hid for a few hours before I went home. He pulls up to my apartment on my Japanese racer drenched in sweat. I asked him if he had been riding for long. It took him a minute to answer, so I continued to talk. I told him if that is what you want, go for it, but I will not be in the mix with her. Then there was Tracy and Sally and Jane.

So, I decided to do my shit, and honey, my shit was downright good. We would have cookouts on the weekends during the summer and invite friends over. This particular day, we had a little get-together at the house. However, a few more items were needed, like beer and chips. I went to the grocery store, walked to the beer section, and I see this tall, dark man looking at me one from the fruit section. I put on the gleaming smile, hum potential. I have never seen him before, so he must be new to town. I was wondering which based. He walks over and introduces himself; they call me Universal, and you are.

I don't care for procrastination, so I made a decision on the stop. Universal, the New Yorker was in my eyesight as a potential lover right now for whenever Joe fucked up again. Yes, bitch, I am planning for your next fuckup.

Universal went his way, and I went mine without any exchange other than our eyes meeting and names. I drove up in the driveway and parked the car, Joe came outside to get the grocery bags with his fine ass. The fire was hot on the grill, our friends were everywhere drinking, and conversing, telling lies. As I was preparing the fish for the grill, adding some more lemon juice to the baby shark that was marinated overnight, I heard a familiar voice. I looked around the corner and stepped a little further into the living-room, just close enough to eavesdrop on the conversation. It was Universal talking to Joe about the woman he saw in the grocery store that was all over his dick.

Well, now Joe was my one and only, we fucked a few times every day, yes, every day. He never licked, sucked or smell…totally all pussy and different positions with his dick being sucked how and when he wanted. I was good with that and never asked for that experience so I never had an organism with him over the nine years. We ended up living together for a few years, but I always kept my apartment just-in-case shit happened. He came home to me every night, and we spent quality time together, I never found him boring, just intriguing. There was a mystery to him and I wanted to know what it was because he just knew he was untouchable. This older woman was after him; she was ten years older and established. So, she piqued his interest, probably some old woman sex antics or voodoo, being she was from Frogmore Island. The land of Dr. Buzzard where you and never eat or drink anything red from the Native Islanders, you will never be the same again.

He was gentle, passionate, and took his time. At 28 years old, he was my first real experience in a long-term relationship. However, I did have boundaries of what I was going to accept and what was intolerable. This older woman was acceptable because he had so much dick; it was enough to share. It was so big I had to always work with it semi-hard. I had to ease on down it, it got hard fast and lasted a long time. I see all the pleasure was his, I experience a hot steamy bath afterwards, *enjoyment of knowing he was inside and that feeling is going to be felt into tomorrow*, and I was in Love. We compromised on a few things, I accepted that he wanted his dick sucked, but I wanted to watch Arsenio Hall Show, so we compromised. He pulls the mattress in the living room in front of the TV. I fixed him a Hennessey on the rocks, three ice cubes, and stirred twice just as he steps out of the shower.

Joe, the relaxed moaner get his dick sucked the way he likes it, I gave him all the oral he could handle with a little baby oil for me to help my fat lips not get in the way of my motion with firmness, lip tight like a pussy, and no teeth contact. Dick has to hit the back of your throat with every thrust back and forth, don't lose contact need to have the continuous flow. I could feel the cum rising up the shaft of his long hard dick, it explodes in my mouth, but I can't let go. He moves my head back and forth like a barnyard chicken taking in his entire massive dick. This is where Sally and Mary could lend a few lips, and I would not have a mind.

It means the head without the brains, the thing I had no control over. Besides, Joe and I had already sat down and established some ground rules. Joe understood me and was the only man I ever told about my childhood. He was willing to kill them all, some were still alive. I explained to him that I saw a few of them suffer and heard a few had a horrible death. I took no joy in telling him this but he was so angry and hurt for what I had experienced. When our relationship approached the eight year and he got out of the

Military things changed. A terrifying storm came, literally and we drove to Rochester New York, his home to his sister home. For some reason he did not want me out of his sight. So, my children and I went with him to Rochester and the storm followed with strong gusting winds but not with the damage you would see in the South. Joe was on his old stomping grounds with his friends and I was among strangers. We stayed longer than expected, a few weeks passed so I applied for an open position at Strong Memorial Hospital in Rochester and got the job. I decided to see how things were going to play out. My children went to school and I went to work, hating that knee-deep snow. Now, he is going back and forth to South Carolina and spending more time with this older woman while we are in the house with his sister and I can feel she does not care for me being with her brother. So, she tells me what he is doing in Carolina. He is no longer with me when it is time to have dinner or go to bed. This mother fucker is taking me for granted. But, shit I am not auguring, complaining or fighting because we don't do that. I set boundaries, save my money and gave him some of my bonus and made plans to leave if he did it one more time. He fucked up, he spent my hard-earned money on the old bitch in South Carolina, bought her a car, while I am catching the bus in the got damn snow. Ugly, just don't do to good. We were supposed to go out a group of us, dressed and waiting at the house to go to a show his nephew was promoting. A call comes in from the ambulance driver, "is this Mr. Lewis wife, Shasha and I responded yes, this is she. Apparently, he gave my name as his wife. The paramedic described his condition and they were not expecting him to not arrive alive to the hospital.

We all rush to the hospital to be by his side and he asks for me only. Half of his right ear was cut off, hi throat was cut from ear to ear, and other defensive cuts on his arms and back but the throat was the worse. Far from a sexual relationship, old people sex but I Loved him. So, I stayed by his side. He had a reaction to the surgical strips on the wound on his throat that swollen up and itched like hell. I held his hand when he slept to keep him from scratching and making it worse. Thank God I had him listed as my spouse and on my insurance. He got the best medical service to include plastic surgery and keloid injections due to scar tissue. After, he recovered and went out to an appointment we left and moved to Tampa Florida without a word as to why. I am sure his sister gave him the details, just as she told me the old woman was pregnant. I really did not like Tampa, I put the children in school and got a job at the Tampa VA. He called a lot and wanted to know where I was. Months passed and I would not tell him my whereabouts. He was so remorseful…yeah right. He went to Beaufort and my mother told him where I was and he showed up at the door. She really loved herself some Joe. She took one look at his feet when she first met him and said "I hope you're not hurting my daughter. He was taken for a moment but just smiled. I was so hurt, this was my biggest pain ever, like being in labor and never birthing the baby. I hated him with a passion and he could not take it. We talked and I told him I would never forgive him for this type of betrayal. He wanted us to reconcile and go back to South Carolina with him, no reconciliation but we did go back to S.C. to my mother. I decided not to accept the job in Tampa instead I accepted a position on Hilton Head

Island until I save enough money to move to Atlanta, Georgia. I worked at a Retirement Home for two months while living with my mother in Beaufort, something I hadn't done since. I think he was seeing old girl still and the baby should be here by now. I heard it was a girl and she already had six kids. He stopped by to see how I was doing, which was great. I was working full time and overtime to get the fuck out of dodge. When he came in and approached me, I stopped him cold in his tracks. I had never been so cold and hard but that bad Gemini came out and my voiced changed, I said I can't stand you or the sight of you stay the fuck out of my life and I don't want to ever see you again. His entire facial expression changed to a damaging hurt that was going to take some time to get those words out of his head. I stayed with my mother for six months and saved enough money to move and my three daughters to Atlanta, Ga. God makes a way, because I did not have a job yet and I just happened to picked up the newspaper to do the puzzle and the Veterans Hospital in Decatur had open positions. I called the number and got interview, hired and a report date in one call. I gave notice to my job, thanked my mother packed on big box and a High School friend drove us to Atlanta, Ga. I rented a car, stayed in the Hotel off of Candler Road next to the interstate and on the bus line for one week. I was searching for an apartment, next to a grocery store and laundry mate in walking distance. I had $450.00 left for an apartment, not asking anyone for shit, just prayed up and determine. I walked into Bosa Nova Apartments on Wesley Chapel road in Decatur, Ga. I had a sincere conversation with the rental agent and I gave her $150.00 deposit for a two-bedroom apartment. I bought an egg crate king size mattress and rented a large TV. A Single parent alone with three daughters 9, 12 and 13 years old. Bosa Nova had frequent shoot outs and roaches but it was only for a minute. Everything else was where I needed it to be. I could to all the amenities I needed and the girl's school. For one year I caught the bus to work, in the pouring down rain wet from head to toe or the burning hot sun. I made a promise to myself that was not going to date another American man no time soon. When I got my income tax return, I bought my first car and we moved to a nice apartment subdivision off of Snap-finger Road in Decatur, Georgia for the next five years. Thank you, Joe, for bringing about the necessary change for the changes. I wasn't dating any military men active or retired only foreigners and Atlanta is a melting pop. In worked one week on day shift and one week on evening shift. My neighbor another single parent watched out for my kids and I watched out for hers. That was the only interest we had in common and both of us moved around the same time. I finally, got back into dating and taking my girls to their father on the weekends and picking them up on Sundays. I was free of worries and could stress a little less. I worked overtime, and for two other agencies one paid daily $300.00 and one weekly. I made a few new friends and the three of us would hang out all night go to work wide awake, none of us drank I guess that was helpful. It has been about two years since I last heard from Joe and again my mother gives him my work number. He is living in Cleveland, Ohio and in Law School. Following his dream, Joe always wanted to be in Politics, he had the thinking mind for the tasks ahead. I was forgiving enough to have a conversation which last for hours. The conversations continue for months as he asked for me to forgive him. He was also asking other women in his past to forgive him as they were calling and exposing him as to how badly he treated them. Apparently, we both have completely different views on what happened in our relationship. He still wanted to see me again. I still said no. I know how to give love but I could not take his love. I was still choosing me and he continued trying to bring us back together. How I saw him was completely different he had damaged the image I built in my mind of how we should have been. A few attempts were made as the years pasted, he loved being around me it was relaxing for Joe, so he needed that while studying for his Bar Exam. I appreciated his time but it wasn't as enjoyable as I anticipated, too many negative memories kept seeping into my mind even thought I keep a smile on my face. Just as it seemed that there might be a chance the devil threw in a monkey wrench Neanderthal bitch into the picture. I accepted his invitation to visit him in Cleveland, Ohio for a week. I had not been on a vacation yet so I was game for a little change in scenery. We had long conversations for hours, he wasn't in at the time but did have a psycho ex that stalk him once in a while...not all the time. No fear for me, he made my travel arrangements and sent me the itinerary... I was on my way the following Friday. It was a realizing there was a pinch of emotions swimming around in my heart for him still. But he had enlightened me a few months earlier that he had adopted the old buzzard bitch from Beaufort six children. All the feelings from the situation in Rochester came down like a flood but I held it back. Thank God for silent dialogue, I and I had it going on all the son of a bitch and mother fucker I could muster up. I can recall feeling happy, extremely happy from my core for a few days in between the mix feelings.

Joe knew to meet me at the airport at 5:00 p.m. something happened with the plane I was initially on and my flight was changed. It wasn't that much of a delay besides I don't like riding on anything with death numbers; 437, 679 and …. The plane was forty-five minutes late and he was so emotional when I called to see where to meet him in the Airport. I could hear the sigh of relief in his voice. I got off the plane and sat in the boarding area for a few minutes and reporters were in the waiting area but I wasn't paying much attention until on approached me and asked if I was afraid. I was startled and sure he could see that on my face because I had no idea what he was talking about. He said the plane that you were supposed to be on crashed…I had one of those moments where I always think everything happens for a reason don't get into the emotions of it, fight it off. All I could say was "no" and walked away. I saw Joe walking and looking around, I called out his name loudly…like I was standing on the back porch of my great-grandmothers shot gun house. He was walking at a fast pace which was unusual, I never witness him moving fasting than a turtle. We embraced each other with a tight hug and kiss on the cheeks. He asked me what I would like to do. Its Cleveland, snow is on the ground and it is still snowing, I just want some good pizza and wings, an easy order. We talked about the plane crash a close near miss. I just wanted to relax and unwind. He had to go back to the office to pick up his brief case in order to complete a summary for a case. The office was only a short distance from his home. He opened the front door and waited for me to enter first as he held the door open, it was a foyer with a table and a large vase filled with white long stem lilies. No rooms downstairs, everything upstairs and the rooms went in a circle with the kitchen in the middle. He gave me a quick tour and where I would be resting my head for the rest of the evening. We heated up the pizza and wings, went back in time sharing memories. Then out of the blue, the doorbell rings, and rings and rings. He looks at me and I look back at him with chicken bone hanging on my bottom lip. I asked in a low voice are you going to answer the door. He put his finger over his mouth jesting for me to be silent. The doorbell ringer did not let up. Loudly, his name was pronounced along with the manly knocking. I said, listen you can go answer the door, he said no she is really crazy and I would have to deal with her and believe me it will be difficult. So, we flipped a coin either he was going to the door or I was…and he did not want me to go. I lost the flip and he answered the door. I told him I was going to stand at the top of the stairs and made no other suggestions. She was enraged and crying and asking him why. I wanted to hear his response, because he told me he wasn't seeing anyone. Good for him, her response was yes you told me it was over…sobbing and I could hear it was the snooty nose crying. I felt some kind-a way for her, but at least he was honest with her, but she could not let go or just did not want to out of rage.

I had not witnessed anything of the sort that was hurriedly running down the way towards Joe and me, as we made it to the departure gate to get on my flight. I heard a faint voice calling out Joe, Joe, Joe, it got closer and closer. He looked at me with his eyes stretched wide and they were already large and beautiful. We stopped dead in our steps and turned to the direction of the voice that was now upon us. I said to Joe, you have a serious stalker, this is not healthy or safe. He suggested I be nice. How, in the hell did she get here so fast, she had to catch a bus and train to get to the airport. What did you do to her for such a display of unstable behavior? As I backed away, I shake my head and she almost ran him over due to the speed she was running...she latched her hands unto his and they walked away. I was awe structed at the shit I just witnessed. Only lesson I could take away was I will never respond like that for a man never.

My flight safely landed at the Atlanta-Hartsfield Airport on time without any mishaps. I was happy to be on my way home with my mind at ease. Joe called around 9 p.m. that night to make sure I was okay and apologize for the turnaround chaotic visit. We stayed in contact for a few years and would visit each other every now and again until it became seldom, emails only, silence then nothing.

Rohan

Mr. Hatman, I met Rogan by way of sister and she was a friend. I thought that he liked me, but after this encounter, I am sure he thought he had a free ticket to Atlanta, nope. Ron and I talk for three months on the phone, wasting my money on prepaid phone cards for this bitch. However, in the beginning, often when a friendship starts in such a manner, feelings blossom very soon. Well, this was the case for Ron. Oh baby, he called me in his deep coarse Jamaica voice. Tell me something about you, and I will tell you anything you want to know about me. Ok, this is a fair game, and I will make it easy for you. Just tell me what you want me to know about you. Baby, I don't want to give it all to you at once, I don't want you to be afraid and throw me back. I smiled and said, "Oh, you are too cute." So, Ron shares how he is a hard worker, four or five *jobs,* and little rest.

A hard-working, hard man with four or five jobs and seldom gets enough rest. He has a 14 years old daughter and a 4 years old son. The daughter is with her mother's parents, and the son is with his mother. He speaks candidly about his mother with so much love, and I admire this in a man. He has two sisters, Karen and Donna, whom I have only spoken with Karen. He often asks questions about my religion and faith; do I believe in God. In this day and time, how could one not believe in God?

Days would pass, but he called every single day sometimes two or three times- good morning, how is your day going, good night. I was *enjoying* the attention and affection, and the old feeling of my heart warming was starting to surface. Shit, they had been dominant for so long. I did not have time for games in my life, too far gone for the nonsense. I entertained his forwardness, to get me as he would put it. I love the sound of his voice; well, any man with an accent turns me on.

We continued to talk; my phone bill was reaching 4 to 5 hundred dollars in a two weeks span. So, I had to cut back. I was lonely and had a few dollars, and now I was broke and happy. I bought a few phone cards for a while, and that worked out perfectly. Ron decided to call me instead of me calling him because the rates were more reasonable on his end.

We continue to talk over the weeks that turned into months, and he never said anything with the slightest sexual tone. For a young man of his years, this was interesting. However, later on, he explained that he would always get "RED" (erected penis) whenever he would talk to me on the phone, and this would keep him up all hours into the night. He said, baby, it just pain-in me so, and takes forever to go.

I stayed away from the sexual tones until one night I was a little on edge myself. I texted him and said, "I am just lying here, playing with myself," wishing you were here. His innocent reply was, "so you are playing with the kids." Oh my God, is he for real? I called him, and we had a good laugh. We laughed often. Our friendship started to feel like we knew each other for a long time. But I sensed that something in the milk is not clean. So, I asked him why you would even consider an older woman to be with instead of someone slightly younger. He explained to me that often, younger men date older women because they have fewer problems compared to a younger woman. They are more into themselves and their needs, money, money, and more money.

Six feet and five inches tall, honey-golden completion, and as sexy as he can be, he seductively moistens his lips, I felt like he was eating something I wanted some of and I was anxiously waiting for him to offer it up. If you could have seen my face...sometimes the simplest visual sexual stimulation can cause a sultry heating moistness to overcome my body suddenly. It made heat rush to my special spot. I wanted him to come and play in my garden and smell my flowers. All I could do was rub my thighs back and forth slowly down to the knees, silently talking to myself. It was like my body was working itself out sweat and all, but I had not moved an inch. I eventually went home alone. I stayed in Negril for a week, it was so damn hot and the air conditioning went out. When maid service arrived, I put in a complaint, she said don't worry it will come back on when the sun sets. I smiled and replied with a thank you. I helped her make up the bed and she left. A thought popped into my head, call Ron so I followed my mind and called him. Hi, can you come over for a while, the room is really hot and it is causing me to sweat in forbidden places. I am going to need your assistance to stay dry. I prefer to be patted dry if you don't mine. No, I don't mind it will be my pleasure. I felt like I was in an African safari movie, nothing but sun and heat and the linen dress I was wearing that draped off of me more than on me was wet and sticking to my body. I heard a knock at the door and it was Ron. I invited him to come in and have a seat. He sat on the bed and watched me as I stood on the balcony watching the waves in the ocean brush up against the rocks. He called me to come to him, come here...please, come here. I said come one time to many so I went and sat on his lap. He began singing "Love won't let me wait" oh my it was as if Luther was in the room. His voice was mesmerizing that dress just slide off without any effort, just drop my arms to my sides instantly gone.

Ron, was gentle as he caressed, kissed and held me in his arms. That lasted for about 30 minutes, I love the gazing in my eye, pushing my hair out of my face to kiss my forehead, enveloping my face in his hands for another kiss. At minute 31 and zero seconds, I was "what in the hell is this" everything was flipped and flopped. He was working hard and over time proving he was worthy. Shit why not, let him...so I let him. Ron, in his strong Jamaican voice, said come on, let me lay you on the edge of the bed. I was wondering, if Stella felt this way when she got her groove back. Well, I was on my way to capturing my groove moment. We laid in bed kissing each other, he was on top and my hips right at the end of the bed. He slowly kisses my lips and gives a gentle bit to my bottom lip and a holding suck. A nibble on my ears and follows down the carotid artery in my neck. He noticed how my body responded to the gentle sucking along the artery on the right side in my neck. It felt like I was having a head organism, the jerking was uncontrollable. That did not slow his role, he moved on down the road to my mouth full of breast with the hard-erect nipples. This is another hot spot for me, damn he was making his way to the jack pot. Now, I am tired from panting and thirsty but I don't want to interrupt the flow. Especially, since he is headed south. Once he hit the spot, a long hoarse sigh passed my lips, my neck was dry. But he was about to quench his thirst. The juices were flowing, the coochie was soaking wet, and I could hear the wondrous noise as his lips pulled it all in. My hands gripped the sheets and pulled them bottom up to the top, it was intense. My thighs caught a case and locked his head in place for a few minutes, he was trying to bury his head deeper and my legs gave way and my hands were not in agreement to hold his head back so they just provided a little gentle guidance. I like a man that will smell, lick and suck, for hours make it hard for me to walk. Damn he gave out of this world head or not having any for a long time "the buildup" made me think he was that good and about taking him home. Shit, this man has skills; he was even building his home, by his self. All I am going to say about the Dick, was I felt the residual a week after returning home. I would have worked with him; he was promising but he made a grave mistake. I heard him tell someone on the phone "I got her". Damn, nope…and never again. I wonder what became of Ron.

Steve

Steve was a darling. Standing 76", muscle-bound, with an olive complexion. Confident in his stride, he walks erected like that proud Marine. I love a tall man; my head normally rests at the base of his breast. I feel so warm and tingly when he wraps his arms around me. Like a smooth drink going down the back of my throat, that stops and heat up my heart before going straight for the coochie.

I was introduced to Steve by Dessa-the Royal bitch of the low country in Beaufort South Carolina. This was in the summer of a few years ago. Steve was active duty and stationed on Parris Island MCRD as a drill Sergeant. I was living in Decatur, Georgia, and working for VAMC as a Geriatric Nurse. We would talk on the phone for hours about work, family, and the issues that followed each. Periodically, I would drive to Beaufort, S.C., to visit my family and spent some time with Steve. I remember we talked like an old married couple. We never spoke of intimacy between the two of us, never saying how I missed you or how much I want you.

There was one concern I had about Steve, but this will be a lifelong secret. Whenever he had some time off or a holiday came around, he would pay me a visit in Atlanta. We would go out to dinner and a movie and talk about his future plans. I can't recall how I truly felt about him during this time because that secret stayed in the front of my mind every time we got together. I was off every weekend, so I went to Beaufort more often than he came to Atlanta. Besides, Beaufort is the beautiful Bay by the Seashore.

This small town is filled with gorgeous greenery, wildflowers, beaches, the best seafood, and a romantic bright starlight sky. The nightlife could be exciting if you enjoyed partying with the Military guys. There are three Military bases, the Naval Station and the Quarter deck Lounge, enlisted club and Officers club on the Air Station, and of course, Paris Island enlisted party spot. Steve was not into any of this, just work and talk. I think maybe he was still stuck in the married zone.

We took long strolls holding hands and walking down the beaches of Hilton Head Island, our shadows casting against the ocean in the moonlit night. All I could hear was the sound of the waves washing into shore and out again. At that moment, I was wishing Steve would lay me gently on the ground, kiss me with his smothering lips, slid his hand under my hips, and just take me like the ocean coming in and going out. Instead, he pulls me closer and places his arm over my shoulder and leads me back to the room.

My every command. Patience is such a good virtue. The following day he called and came over for a short while, and later that evening, he drove us to Savannah, Georgia, for dinner on the waterfront. We shared a breath-taking evening of good foods, spirits, and each other company. We got acquainted, shared life experiences and childhood memories. It felt as if I had known him all my life. For the next six to eight months, we spent a lot of time together. It got to the point where I had the keys to his house and vehicle. I was the first person he saw in the morning and the beautiful face he saw when our heads rest next to each other at night. Steve retired from the Military and moved to Atlanta, Ga. I got to see him more frequently and we did have a few intimate encounters before his retirement. But we were more friends than lovers. He experiences a bad break up where his wife left him and took the kids while he was in Drill training. He talked about it often and was having a hard time healing. He never shared the reasons she left and I did not question him. He appeared to be a good man ... guess he wasn't for her. So, I am going to keep his secret and not say much about the sex. He didn't seem to be the type that was in the streets chasing water falls. We were young and the more we dated I observed that he had some control issues. He wanted to control me, nope not going to work. He had no leverage; the sex was bland...so I gradually put distance between the two of us until I hadn't seen him in a few years. Since he was a Veteran and in Atlanta, we ran into each other in the hallway at the VAMC. We instantly recognized each other, talk a little and shared numbers to catch up on life later. He was still very handsome, but my heart did not beat fast nor did my coochie jump or got moist. I smile and walked away to return to my work area. By the weekend Steve called and wanted to meet up at his place. I was okay with the arrangement and agreed to meet him at his place. I did not have any high hopes of anything taking off between us because of his secret. He was a little thicker and muscular really looking good. Steve, wanted to be intimate, he was the let's make Love man, not let's fuck or can we have sex.

I am usually working two or three jobs, in school, and taking care of six children. Therefore, a few years might past by and I am not sexually involved. You might wonder how can that be…well it happens. So, again…yes Steve and I made love that night but it was nothing explosive. It wasn't as I remembered, it was better and it should be as improvement should come with time… except in Joe's case. Along with the thicker muscular look, the dick width had increased. In silent dialogue with myself, which I often do… damn he must have found that African root that increases the blood flow to make his junk larger. Honey, I got up on boy. I was riding, riding and riding. I was surprised that he was up so long, but it felt so good. I did not want him to help at all, just let me ride in peace. I laid my head down on his chest, felt as if I was taking one step at a time climbing a ladder higher and higher. Just before I reached the top looked up to how much further I had to go and saw him looking down at me. This was the moment I felt like a hungry gremlin and stop. I was riding him nonstop like I was starving, damn I got off…off of him. We hung out a few more times but no more making Love. I still see him in the Hospital ever so often when he has an appointment, he stops in to say hello.

Chief Bob

I have known the Chief for more than 25 years, we became good friends after a few weeks of his arrival to Atlanta, Georgia from Charleston South Carolina after a lengthy divorce he decided to relocate. He caught my eyes one evening as I getting ready to leave work and he was doing his location checks in the building. He spoke, hello, how are you? My name is Bob, I am new to Atlanta and the VAMC. Shasha, replied was, "hi I am great" as she measured him up from mid waist front view to feet and back to his face in that order. She was attracted to him from the first introduction. Every day she worked he would stop by her unit while on his rounds and talk while she worked for a few hours. Just small talk, he had that southern drawl you knew he lived by water for a long time. He had that Military marching walk, looked delicious in that uniform, tall and dark with a shiny bald head and a sneaky smile that rang out loud, come lay with me if you want. During our talks, my body was talking to me but I wasn't listening, I just entertained the conversation and moved on. I listened to his relationship issues from the ex-wife to the pussies at work that he got with or was chasing him. My work area became a constant hideout from one big grizzle woman, he was afraid of her. I would be too. She was larger in width and at least two inches taller, you could hear her coming down the hallway. It started to seem like I was his personal therapist but I did not have to say much. The feeling remained the same but to reactions just a listening ear. After a few years, our relationship continued the same as usual. Talk, talk, and more talking, by now I am giving my opinion. First, you will be marrying the woman you leave at your house every day you come to work. He was determined that he will never get married again. She got pregnant and all his other children were teenagers, so he felt some kind of way about the pregnancy but she was keeping the baby. The man that was determined to never get married again due to a bad divorce was married in a matter of months. Ok, he felt she got him but I pointed out how he had an equal part in the situation. Bob and I were still good friends and he continued to visit 15 years, it was his Birthday and he came by my office and asked for a Birthday hug. It dawned on both of us that we have never touched each other and he defiantly deserved a hug. So, we shared a nice long hug between friends. It was this day that he shared he had a crush on me since the first day we meet. Now, it was sitting down time because I was shocked. I said to Bob, I had no idea how you felt … but I have had a crush on you just as long. He wanted to know why I never said anything to him about how I felt. I sadly, explained that you always came to see me and wanted my advice which I willing gave. You always spoke of your feeling for other women and I did not see an opening in your life for me. It was a wow moment. We continued with our special relationship as I was also friends with his now current wife. Which, she knew of our friendship before they started dating, had the baby and got married. She, wasn't worried about me, just other women that were chasing him. With the type of friendship, we had I asked him bluntly, why do you mess around with women in the same place your wife works and it gets back to her. He asks me if I believed

everything I heard and I said no. But your wife approached one woman and threatened her and I saw how that particular woman acts in your presence. It is just passing my 20th year and his birthday is approaching it is November already. The man I admired for over 20 years just told me he had been separated from his wife for the past four months. Bob called and said, "Hello, so you're at work today?" in a deep sensuous voice. He has the voice that makes you wet your panties or go crouch less. So, I replied, "yes, stranger, I thought you forgot about us?" "Bob, responded how can I forget the woman that has been teasing me for the last 20 years? How long are you going to be at work? Probably, two more hours or however long it takes you to run to me." "Okay, see you at three o'clock."
It is a slow day in the office. I made a few calls to catch up with friends and family, read my emails, and thought about Bob. He has been my inspiration to come to work; just the anticipation of seeing him in the hallway was organismic.

The marriage is on the rocks, the wife has moved out and he is anticipating that she is filing for a divorce. Yet, she still comes over and break up shit in the house looking for the other Bitch ever so often yelling and screaming "where the bitch at where is she"? I just had to ask, what is it that drives these women crazy? He got his Birthday hug and left with a smile without giving me an answer. I heard about him and the new woman dating, bring him lunch, picking out his new home and decorating and moving in with her daughter. Got damn, I thought in that silent dialogue again, this could have been my time. We still talked but not as often he was really into her. Which was different even from the last two relationships with the wives before they were wives. This was a huge spark; he was hook on enough to cut out the other options. This lasted for about 5 years and ended, he said she ended it but he was going to wait on her. So, he invites me over to the new house for thanksgiving weekend to talk and watch Western movies…the house that she is no longer at because she went back to her husband…damn… right. Isn't that some shit but he is still waiting on her, so I am listening not drinking? I can see he is hurting and hear it in his voice as he talks about her and her daughter. He has had a few drinks to many. Glass still in his hand and a few more drinks drowning sorrow, I am listening. He said, you could have been my wife but you did not put forth any effort. I told him, out of respect for myself and your wife, ex-wife I was going to do that. Shit, where was your effort? He said I am showing you now…but no he wasn't. He was bleeding his heart out about the woman that left him with the pretense of returning. I want to be your first choice not your second or third or you are at a cross roads in deciding who you want to be with and it is taking you months. If that is how you are rolling take me out of the equation. Bob, feeling good and exploring all his pinned-up emotions decides to show me where I will be sleeping but didn't hesitate to make an offer to share his bed. Oh girl, did an awesome job with the decorations it was warm, inviting and had a masculine touch. I took a long hot shower, did all my personal hygiene stuff and asked him for one of his shirts to sleep in. All he had on was some pajama bottoms and no shirt, showing off his pecks and yes, they were well formed. I told him I would like to sleep in his bed and we could talk and cuddle. I don't care for drunk sex, so that wasn't happening but the sleeping arrangement was fine. We laid in bed talking about sex and he thought he could .get me to take part in what he wanted. I wasn't feeling him sexually and probably because he was still sitting on the same stoop when it came to his relationships. He was determined to get me to partake but I stood my ground to a certain point. There was a little wrestling, I like to pretend you are taking it forcefully. But we both decided to stop and I decided to show him a trick. My God, did he enjoy the trick, my God I just had to ask what have you been doing with the women you have been dealing with. It's nothing like I just did with my hands he ever experiences. After I held it in my hands, I had a few more questions for instance, again what is it that drives the women crazy? He said it is not the size it is what happens once you are inside the coochie. Humm, okay then, I will let that rest right there. It must have been God that kept us apart all these years until now...thank God. I moved on and we still stayed in contact sometimes at work, more on the phone than before. No talk of sex, but when I saw him at work, I always gave him that special hand signal related to our secret. I got the biggest smile in return. He was divorced and his ex-wife was retired from the VAMC before I spent the night. As we approached the 25th year and his Birthday was approaching he came back for his final hug in November as he was retiring in January 2020. Wrapped tightly in his arms, he whispered in my ears "you could have been my wife" and I had that silent dialogue once again, "man you don't eat pussy, I need my coochie licked, sucked and smelled by my man."

Secret Lover

It is so strange how things happen in life, especially when you least expect something to go down. It was the weekend before Father's Day 2010; I was so stressed between work, school and a Data Analysis class, 15 kids, and the dog. I was staying late at work due to my final week in class and ready to throw the towel in, and wherever it landed was just fine. I thought by staying at work late to finish up on some assignments, the children would be asleep by the time I arrived home. To my surprise, the children were knocked out, but Rocky, my dog, was still up. I was facing the worse ten weeks I have ever experienced in years in class, but I wanted my Ph.D. in Psychology.

To start, my advisor registered me the same day classes started and dropped a class that I did not need. Meanwhile, she was trying to explain I would have enough time to catch-up with my classwork, not what I wanted to hear. I was supposed to get the computer program PSAW that I never heard of before, now and know how to use this product two weeks before the course starts, but here I am today, starting.

 Let me introduce you to Turmoil, we go way back and have known each other very well; we could actually be related in some form, probably a past life. I received the program three weeks after the start date of the class, the adapter burned out, and the children put a password on my computer that took a week to get off. Once I received the program, I had trouble getting the licensure validated or verified. I was working hard to try and complete the 20 PSAW assignments and the ten-course room assignments. My nerves were a wreck. This is one of my dry spells no Dick and very little vibrator usage.

Innocently, I suggest to a friend that he should let me be his roommate for the next five days. Meanwhile, his two daughters would be out of town with their auntie. I could cook his meals for those days, get some well-deserved rest, and do a little writing. Both of our blood pressures would have time to go down. Also, if he had time, he could give me a few swimming lessons. To my surprise and I was surprised that he said, okay, I'll see you on Wednesday when I return from New York. As part of our deal, he indicated that I would be doing all the driving to and from work. I was thinking, this really sounds awesome, so it was a sealed deal. I deserved a break from my wonderful life of never-ending love and affection from the children and Rocky.

The weekend shot by fast as lightning speed, I was excited to be out of the house and not have to pay an arm and a leg for the Hilton. Usually, I spent my ME time at the Hilton in Atlanta next to Hartsfield- Jackson Airport. The view from the 13th floor is a dream. Well, due to a few unforeseen interruptions from my family, all fifteen of them and Rocky, I could not make it to his home before Friday. He seemed a little disappointed that I was not coming over until Friday evening. his great big smile slowly melted away as if he was frosty the snowman and summer caught him off guard.

Friday in the morning, I woke up, bags packed the night before. I took one uniform, tennis shoes, black heels, a black linen sundress, and a few sexy delicate. I was not really expecting to go out anywhere. Besides, I was staying in his upstairs apartment and not disturbing anyone. We went about our day at work, nothing interesting happened other than the patients. Anticipating when 4:30 pm will finally get here, the day was lingering. So, I did a few of my assignments with only one day left to finish all of them. My plans were to get to his home, shower, cook dinner, and then pick up where I stopped with the assignments.

He reminded me of our deal, and I informed him it was okay, and that I remembered. He smiled and walked away. His smile is so sexy. The shift ended. I went down the back stairs and put my bags in his car. He had parked close to the building at the back entrance. He was driving a sporty royal blue Mercedes SUV. He opened the door and placed my bags in the rear seat as I walked around to the driver's side and placed my little rump there comfortably. We pulled out of the parking lot for a quiet weekend. We laughed and talked all the way to his home, 45 minutes *enjoyable* drive. Beforehand, I parked my champagne two-door convertible Lexus coupe in the doctor's garage at the hospital.

He wants to be my husband, my second husband, my last husband, Humm. He is an overall nice man, (Scorpio) loves the ground I walk on, until he doesn't get his way. He likes things his way. He's not going to do anything for you unless it is going to be beneficial to him in some way. He did everything for me with expectations of eating my coochie. Wash and iron my clothes, cook dinner or buy it mostly on weekends, with expectations of licking and sucking and smelling my coochie. Cleaned the tub and prepared my bath afterward in hopes of licking and sucking my now cleaner, hot moist coochie. He catered to me, before the marriage regardless, after the marriage this man was something extra. It took about 18 months before he pops the question, after knowing me for 15 years. I told him I would be seeing other people and spending less time with him. He was a homebody no interest in nothing but cleaning, eating chicken and licking, sucking and smelling my coochie. He had a nice size dick, and it got hard, but it would flop if the coochie got to close....what the fuck. Just say eat coochie, and he gets hard as a rock like it was conditioned to recognize those words, like Pavlov experiment with the rat with the cheese. I stayed in curiosity mode, questioning the behavior. I was forward and asked him if he was bi-sexual or gay, and he said no. Still, not *enough* to satisfy my curiosity. Therefore I started observing him more. Do you have a war injury? Were you sexually traumatized in the Military? He simply said no. Something just was not right, and I asked millions of questions. Until, he asked, is this marriage going to be all questions? This motherfucker told me that he is slow, mentally slow. That has nothing to do with dick and pussy issues. If anything, they are overly sensitive from not getting any.

He continued to prepare me for bedding me down. Husband, home all day, I guess. After I get in the bathtub, I would call him to come and wash my back, and he was always willing. He could soap up a few spots he expected to visit later on. He ran the wet towel between my legs and asked if he could get a kiss. I said no, and he left out and sat on the bed watching TV. I called him back, you missed a spot, and he said where. I got up out of the tub of hot water for my slow husband and sat on the side, he was already on his knees, and I pull his head towards my thighs, smoke from the hot water rising up between us. I guide his head until I have had enough, besides it was just a taste. I smile and slide back in the tub of hot water; he says, "damn," and I said, "later on, Hun."

For some reason, the desire wasn't there. He asked to massage my feet. I said yes, of course, he warms the oil and does an awesome job of relaxing me. The husband makes it all the way to my knees. "Hold up". You said feet, and now you are passing my knees, where are you going? He laughs, and I rolled over. Maybe, his asking before doing is the problem. Shit, just do it. But again, knowing me, it is probably best for him to ask before doing.

There are so many things we have never done. We never shared a long kiss, shit a single kiss. You know the one on the lips, and the tongues play around a little bit. I was okay with that because he dribbled a lot. In or out of bed, just watching TV, I could see the glycerin drool coming down the corner of his mouth. So, I would ask, "what is wrong with you? Why are you drooling?" He said, "I just want a lick, a suck, a smell, or suck your nipples." My thoughts were this is unusual and cute, so I let him have some nipples, put me right to sleep.

He wasn't a hugging husband, it felt awkward and looked awkward, and someone else was telling him to hug his wife. The hug was as if someone had just punched him in his stomach, and he had to bend over in pain.

All he wanted was a lick, a suck, a smell, or suck on my nipples, for me that was not enough anymore. I never sucked his dick, never felt the move to, and he never asked, but he begged for the touch of my hands, it felt better than his. I felt that there was a distance between us, and I did not like the feeling. So, I would go to my house when I started feeling unwanted. How can you be married and still live as if you are a single individual, I felt as if we are never together, no oneness. Everyone came before me, his friends, family, and even the neighbors. I got tired of being last and brought it to his attention. What did he say? Not a got damn thing.

He had to have everything his way, so I moved into the direction of going out and socializing, spending more time with myself and going back to college. I know my worth, but he did not recognize it, sadly.

He told me I was smarter than him, I could articulate better than him, I just knew what to say, and he could not communicate in the same manner. I told him that it doesn't matter, just talk to me. But I still went on with my decision to work on me. I wouldn't go see him for two to three months at a time, sometimes longer. When he realized I was seeing someone else, he decided to propose.

I was at a Union training at the Hilton downtown Atlanta, Georgia, for a week. He dropped me off and took my bags to my room and left. On the last day of the training, he calls and invites me to dinner at Ruth's Chris Steakhouse. I was tired and said no, another time. I already had a reservation at the Hilton in Charleston, South Carolina for the weekend. I thought about his invite and got upset, this mother fucking has known me all these years and never went to a restaurant that the price list was more than Red Lobster. The only time I have dined at Ruth's Chris was when I took myself or on a business dinner.

So, I put two and two together that he wants to propose. The following week we talk about the dinner invite, and he shares that he had invited me because he was going to propose and had a ring. I said, yeah, right, all in one week. Where is the ring, he said he took it back, ok? A few weeks passed, and I am still keeping my distance, and he calls inviting me to dinner again after work this time. I said, ok, but it will be my treat at Longhorn. It is less than a mile from my job.

He came right at 4:30 p.m. as I was getting off work, and he picked me up in front of the Hospital. He was dressed like he had an appointment, head shiningly bald, rose quartz color shirt new, black slacks fitting, and shiny shoes. He laughed nervously; I asked him if he was okay. He said

yes, I added that I did not have any bad news for him, and he smiled again. He was just not himself, we ordered dinner, and he got up to go to the restroom, still, could not figure out why he was so nervous. As I was looking at my phone and responded to a text, I turned around, and he was shockingly on his knees, holding a black velvet ring box.
I was really speechless to the point that I said, are you sure? Then while he was still on one knee and the waiter was so excited for me, to the point that he was hopping and jumping around like he said yes. I had other thoughts going on in my head. This is really a no, why would you ask me this in front of these strange people, where I can't say no because I don't want to crush you? How dare you ask me now when you think or know there is someone else?

It was a beautiful ring, and he took me straight to the jewelry store he bought it from because it was a little tight. It took about two weeks to come back. The salesperson said the two of them, and his granddaughter helped pick out the first ring. They were concerned when he came back but happy to see that he returned it and chose another. The engagement lasted for 30 days. I saw Doc at least twice during that time, around day 31, I reached out to Doc. I got no response, he ghosted me for more than a month. One day, the Husband to be pops up for lunch. Then he says, "let's get married today; (feeling a little like Al Green I guess) let's just go downtown to the courthouse." Well, what I wanted wasn't responding, and I felt Doc had moved on. So, I said ok, and we went to the courthouse with my daughter on my lunch break.

The Judge explains how the process works. You have fast and very fast. Very fast lasted five minutes and we went first. We got a very fast process, and I was back at work with five minutes to spare, married. Should have known it really wasn't going to work, when he was so nervous and shaking the judge put the ring on my finger…what the fuck was that about?

I was thinking about Doc and my happiness, guess it just wasn't in the cards. Well, no wedding night bliss or sex, I was drained. Weeks went by, and he got a little more controlling, wanting to take me to work and pick me up. Why must it be a trust thing? I was starting to feel sick, just being in his presence. My body was telling me he is not the one. I would get the hiccups and a headache every night around 10 p.m. I had to even go to the hospital multiple times. I was not sick at work or at my house, only when I am with him.

I went to work, Doc's brother asked me if it was true, and I said, "What?" "That you got married," I said, "yes, but let me tell him." Doc started calling, asking if I miss him, and when could he see me. Well, it has been a minute, *but by him calling to ask I knew his brother told him what took place.* So, I planned on going to see him, and I did, back to the same location where we met. I Love him internally, and I can't let go. I let him know that I am in town and the room number. He said he will be over when he gets off work at 7:00 p.m. I took a shower and slipped into this little red linen dress. No, towel or special preparation this time. No dinner was waiting, no king size bed but a double because I came to tell him what happened and how it happened.

He walks in with a big bag, and he said, "This is for you, I think congratulations are in order. Why? Why did you do it? Just tell me why? Why are you giving up all of this?" Doc leans over me as I sat on the bed. He comes in closer and kisses me, all of this, you are just going to let it go. I said no, I thought you were gone. I am sorry, we laid in bed fully clothed and held each other for hours with tears rolling down both our cheeks. I only wanted to be with him, and he was sorry that he could not offer me what the husband has to offer. I tried to explain mistakes happen, but I was in love with him. Weeks and months went by, I would just show up, and he would come. But in December of 2018, he said, "come on, let me know when you arrive." I did the usual, let him know I was in town. I was heartbroken for this was the first time he didn't show. I had already filed for the divorce about a year prior, and he knew this.

I got updates on him periodically when I asked his brother, and now he was in a committed relationship. Wow, my divorce was final Jan 8, 2019, and I never told anyone. I wish him the best. However, every 3 or 4 months, I will send him a song that says I am missing you. The last text I received from him was July 2019, "I just want you to know that I love you." I respond back, I know and I Love you too. Maybe I should tell him I am divorced, but it probably won't matter. My heart wants him, but I don't want to feel that pain ever again. I still send a text message when I experience a moment of weakness just to let him know he crosses my mind (i.e., March 2020).

But, after a year of this roller coaster ride, I asked for a divorce, we were better friends than husband and wife. I know he holds resentment and a little animosity but will take me back in a blink if that was ever what I wanted.

How could I deprive myself after Doc? I couldn't. Did I want some more of Doc? Yes, I did. He gave me a look when those words rolled off my lips and landed in his audio range. He did not want a divorce, but I told him I wasn't happy. I am sure he was boiling with anger; I could see those beady little eyes roll closer to his nose like a criminal ready to attack, but all he did was sigh. It could have been a sign of relief because he was glad, I was asking him. Over a year had passed, and I guess I asked at the right time and made reference a few times. I reiterated that while I wasn't asking for anything from him, it would be a good time to go to the courthouse and sign the divorce papers. He said if that's what I wanted; he will do it for me. He never talked much unless I insisted, and it got us nowhere. I have known him for more than 15 years. He has his mean moments, until I show him, I don't need anything from him. Then he wants to invite me over for dinner and a movie or a drive to the Casino, or Florida or New York. No, thank you just got back from a long trip just going to stay home and rest. Hey he says…if only you knew how much I love and miss you.

I meet this old lady by way of a co-worker, her name was Ms. Mary she was a Prophet in her Church. She was very helpful to me during this stage of my life as she was my listening ear. I never shared what was going on with me to my family, I kept it all tucked away inside. She gave me Bible verses to read related whatever I was going through at the time. I really appreciated her coming into my life when she did. Ms. Mary gave me a glimpse of my future. She said a Rob, Ron, or Roger will soon appear and be good for me a helper. But I don't know anyone by these names, but I was careful on the lookout for any man with these three to five letters of the alphabet. Once you pass a certain age, things change that isn't related to gravity descending. I started to look at my life in a different light. Once I realized that my feet are closer to the grave rather than that cradle, and if I did not make some drastic changes, that would be the ultimate outcome, just sooner than I could anticipate. My life appears to have always been in search of something, and I will get back to that in a moment. I am one of those individuals that can honestly say, "if I do a, b, and c, I know "e" will happen." I stopped cold turkey with men and relationships and worked on me.

I knew I needed some overhauling, and this was too much for a therapist; believe it when I say I tried. I felt like my clients, and this is not going to work, okay, I know how to do this, my self- talk. The worse was when I helped someone I loved, and they walked out. But it was my expectation that more would come from the relationship because of my sacrifices. What showed up was a rude awaking, heartache, and frustrations. After the second week

of the marriage, I picked up a set of divorce papers for ten
dollars from the DeKalb county courthouse and placed it
under my bed in a box.

Waiting until I had enough, I completed a small section at a
time, it took two years before the papers and I walked hand
in hand into the court clerk's office for filing; husband #1.
This was the best seventy-five dollars I had ever spent. My
five minutes of insanity was finally over, and all he wanted
was his name back. For lack of better words, I said (place
whatever words you would like here) "...., ..." You can
have your name back when you pay for the name change.
This man really loves his name, so I kept it out of spite.
Got married a second time and still kept the first husband
name. There was really no real commotion other than with
myself and the life choices I had constantly made over and
over. So, I looked to God and asked questions, and seek
comfort in him and not man.

I often got answers to my question sometimes so fast it was
scary. I have always been a praying individual since a little
girl, remembering my talks with God at such a tender age,
and to see his work in my life. As a result, today is mind-
blowing. So, after the divorce, we still communicated, and
he would stop by and visit. For some reason, he still
considered us to be husband and wife. Pius said, "if I ever
catch you with another man, we are finished." Wow, how
cute. Bismarck, my dear friend at that time came over. Not
feeling well, lying in bed bundled up, Bismarck sat at the
foot of the bed on the right. To my surprise, Pius showed
up, with his little girl in his arms, and sat on the left side of

the bed at the foot. I watched as the two men made faces at each other as one had more power than the other to sit on either side of my bed.

A few hours of silence and the sit-out was over, Pius decided to leave. As he was walking down the stairs, I escorted him to the door. He reminded me of my failure; he caught me with another man, so we were through. I said boy you have made my day, it was the funniest thing I had ever heard, but he was serious, I could see it in his face. Bismarck, Doctor of no commitment even though he has passed the USMLA exams he studied so hard for every day.

I was already a student at the community college, so I profoundly turned to my studies Bismarck was an inspiration and my tutor. I was going to work during the day and classes at night sometimes until eleven o'clock it was so taxing. So tired from family, work, and school, I resorted to taking naps in the car in-between classes, I was on a mission.

Men were outlawed until I finished working on me. Psychology became my best friend, and then I switched my major from Nursing to Psychology. However, there were a few circumstances that had a hand in that play as well. I took everything that was thrown my way and turned it around for good. I always focused on the lesson I was learning, and I was aware that a few lessons were repeated over and over. At this point, I asked God to give me what he wanted me to learn in the simplest form because I knew

I was not getting it. I prayed that he wanted to show me anything I needed to know, to please do it while I was asleep. Let my dreams give me my answers.

Now, I can just ask a question and go to sleep or just go to sleep, and when I wake up, the answer is there. Sometimes I get clarity from a Pastor or friends, but it is usually in line with my thoughts. Yet, still, processing my past relations and what I no longer want, as I have learned from those relationships, they gave me all that I did not want. Love is what? I often ask the lover that cheats, that is never there, the one that only his needs are met. I was selfless and gave unconditional genuine love and affection. All I got in return was a knot in the pit of my stomach, the love diet, can't eat, can't sleep, and just as you are coming up out of the hole, he's back. Out of love, you feel as if you are like the roach in the dark, lights come on they run for cover, lights off they back in again and again. Did not have to look to Pius to act in that light, he had what he wanted, so he was out there living it up, women, money cars, and I was boiling, feeling used up again.

I listened as he often requested, just listen. I listened to him, understood him more, and was happy that he treated me the way he did. It kept me from a lot of trouble and more heartache because I did not know what was going on. I was thankful in the end that he kept me at a safe distance and said no, or he could not tell me what was going on. I had a wow moment after a few other instances, and I realized that he really does care, even enough to show up when I was not expecting him.

Years rolled by fast, children grow, and some parents go to jail. Well, what can I say; shit happens to all of us?

In my prayers, I ask God to keep evil away from me so that I may cause no pain. This is my everyday prayer, and I wonder what would happen if I did not ask this. Then I stopped wondering because I would get that answer as well. Life *journey* has been a laundry list of trials and tribulations; at times, it has been too much. I ask God, is all this for me, is this not too much. God, I know you see me here; this is too much, I know you said you would not give us more than we can handle, yet, God I think you miscounted on my part. This bundle I am carrying is surely heavy, I can hardly make it up the hill, but I carried on. I see no help in sight.

In my blindness I did not realize at the time, his work in all parts of my life. Mistakes were my building blocks, from my parents, grandparents, and great-grandparents. The lessons started, and the neighbors helped out in their own special way; you know it takes a village to raise a child. It seems like it was pure hell raising Shasha, but I like the scent of the rose in full bloom. My blossom is enthralling to the sense of smell, and it can cause you to take a deep breath and draw it all in, engrossing in its beauty.

I did not like myself much as a child, yet, I liked the appearance of my father that was in me. This made me different from all others. I saw him in my face, my long legs, and far-reaching arms. I saw him in my walk and mild manners. I saw him, and then he faded away, piece by piece until all I could recall was his big feet and the wingtip shoes he wore and the style of suits he wore. Everything I knew of him was gone except that which dressed him… his clothes. I felt my life was about not having love… there wasn't any for me for some evil reason. Remember, this was too much for the therapist, and childhood is usually the area to blame when all is wrong in your adult life. So too soon to blame right now, just watch as things continue to unfold.

As I am more observant of things going on around me, I know now it is God's hands at work more each day. A ninety-year-old woman made time for me on Sunday evenings after her Church service. I made notes in my dream *journal*, of her suggestions and words of wisdom. She told me that I would meet a man, that will do the same work as I do, he will be tall, dark, and offer me his scepter. His name would have these letters Ron, Roger, Rob.

More than 15 years have passed, and still no one until November 19, 2012. The notion that this prophecy is finally coming true, I have been waiting and watching. Timing and the steps it took for this moment to finally show up in the midst of all my waiting and hoping and wishing and asking God to send him. I realize that all those other times were not the right times. Too many things were going on in my life. I was evolving and shaping myself with God; he had his hands on me. I kept going through it, going through it, going through it. Well, the old lady said, 'dear, you have nothing to worry about. Your life is blessed."

I told her about a dream I had of her in a beautiful garden, and she had so much to tell people and so little time in life. She was forthcoming in sharing that she was worried about how to reach all the people she needed to help still. We conversed back and forth for more than a year. Until one winter morning, I decided to call her before church because I kept dreaming of her wanting me to come to visit her in Florida. Weeks went by and no answer, I got worried and called my friend that we had in common. She informed me that the old lady had died a few weeks earlier, which was when my dreams of her started. Mrs. Green died in her kitchen; she was found standing at the kitchen sink as if she was washing dishes. She never fell down.

Even though Ms. Green was gone, someone else showed up with the same message. Mrs. Cotton, a younger white female, I meet in Kentucky while visiting a friend. She told me a young man was causing me some trouble, my brother. She repeats word for word, what Ms. Green from Florida had said years earlier. A sense of ease came over me, some relief in knowing things are going to get better. This time I had a list of what was to come, and I marked each off like a bucket list as each came to pass. November 19, 2012, I was only left with two things on my list, and they could come together. Ron, Roger, or Rob, who could this man possibly be? Maybe I have already encountered his presence.
I have not met this man as of yet, but I have heard of him. Wishful thinking, nope the real deal, he will arrive soon, and I can feel it in my loins.

When talking with Saniyah, she told me of this man coming to town two weeks ago. Something in me sparked an interest. Then she followed by telling me of his arrival, then her cleaning his room the next day and how friendly and talkative he was. Samiyah said, "Mommy, he is your kind of man," I said, "really? Tell me more." "He is tall, dark, with a salt/pepper goatee, nice athlete builds, and very apologetic. He is single." then I informed her that this is a window open by God, don't let it pass, everything happens for a reason. Now, put me in the mix when you talk to him again. Another week passes, and she does not have his room, but she is armed it the opportunity should present itself once again.

And yes, it did, the same week on that Sunday morning she texted and said, mommy, I gave him your number, and he asked if you could cook. I told him sure; she is really a good cook. Miracle man wanted to know more, "when last your parents went out together," Samiyah replied 34 years ago. My mom does not really like him, but they are friends. Miracle man then asked about her name, and I told him but that she was divorced. Well, small world it is this miracle man knows my ex-husband, no damper for me. He is an ex-husband of almost ten years, water under the bridge. Miracle man also enquired about my profession. She indicated that he was looking for a five-bedroom house with a two-car garage.

This man was Prophesized to be in my life by four different people in four different states at four different times in my life. So, I continue to work on me, and I worked, and I worked. Forgiving, letting go, and moving through it and moving on out of the storm, this is an ordeal. I strongly believe you have to move through it to get to it, but my God, My God, it is hard. As of now, I am just waiting on the call that I know is coming very soon. I use to hear people say you know when it is right, and I wondered how is that so. I have never felt like that about any man. Now just the description of this man sets me on fire. I am anticipating him contacting me as if I am going to the Prom for the first time. I cooked dinner yesterday, just because today one of my co-workers suggested I cook dinner every day until he arrives.

I explain this feeling as if you are trying a new dessert. It sounds good, looks good, but you have to taste it to know you want that dessert. You can prepare that dessert. I have followed the instructions for years in preparation for getting this well-deserved dessert, damn-it it's my dessert. I don't feel afraid or uneasy. It seems like I am waiting on someone I have known for a while. What am I going to do when I meet him? What will I say? I think I will say it's been a long time. Finally, it is nice to make your acquaintance?

Four hours

I am going to Beaufort for the weekend and hang out at the clubs. Okay, there is only one back in the woods, down a long bumpy dirt road, Studio 7. Beaufort is a military town in South Carolina on the coast, lots of water, available single and married Marines, my favorite, and a few Sailors. The most attractive and adventurous place to be is on base man watching — all sorts of men, from enlisted to Officers, a nice little candy shop.

I should arrive at about 9 p.m., it is a four-hour drive, and now it is about 5 p.m. usually I stop in Augusta, Georgia off of Washington Road for gas, this is enough to get me to Beaufort, my destination. It is a beautiful summer evening at about 83 degrees in Hot Atlanta. I would probably have more fun here in Atlanta, but I really miss the warm sunshine, beaches and pool of men as my playmates. It is always inspiring to be able to pick one man out of twenty, weaning out the happy guys, rather than vis-versa on the scene in Atlanta. The happy guys will definitely give you a run for your money, "no honey, I think he is on my side."
I am going to take my time, just me and my music, crushing these backwoods roads into the Savannah River Plant. This is the scariest place to drive alone. Two-lane highway, with huge trucks, exits to the side with chain locked gates, that leads into a dreary chemical plant; like you are in a horror movie and the man in the truck is pulling up to run your car off the road. It is most alluring as I keep an eye out for the possible UFO's that may land any second now. Just don't let them snatch me up before I get to

Beaufort, where I know there are street lights. This drive helps with keeping my mind sharp and provides a little playtime with the deer's and my cursing, oh shit, I just missed hitting that one. Weaving back and forth, dodging dears running across the road, and I am not about to neither slow down so much nor come to a complete stop.

The ride is always peaceful, a good way to distress. Yet, I needed this after a long week of double shifts at the VA, chasing people whose minds are on the outskirts of town, waiting on them to find their way back. In addition to the mental challenges of the mentally challenged, I find myself cleaning and ducking behind doors out of the line of fire of shit balls. But I *enjoy* what I do, believe me, I really do.
I think I will stop off by my mother's house first, for a few minutes, swing by Jennifer, Joyce, and Sharon. Listening to their lies a short while, and see my granny, the queen of the family. She has the real deal on the family and neighborhood folks — the latest news on who slept with whose husband, wife, or other men. Last, but not least is Uncle Lonnie, Mack daddy stuck in 1970. Pockets loaded with wallets, padding his ass, wow. I look at my family, and wonder with amazement, how could I have chosen this plan with God for my life on this plain. My reward in Heaven must be astronomical.

I ponder in my mind what exit to take Yemassee, which is about 45 minutes from Beaufort or Coosawhatchie. Both are very small towns, blink, and it is gone. As a little girl, my sister Joyce and I waited on the train to go to New York with our great-grandmother many times in Yemassee. Yet, we spent a lot of time in Coosawhatchie, since that was our first stop, traveling from New York. The only reminder from the past that remains is the tracks that I drive across on my way home. I can recall playing in the streets, going to the corner store, or the juke joint for Mama, or getting a cold soda pop or a nickel pickle. Where did the time go, the buildings of yesterday still standing but no one watching, but me and my memories?

Approaching the last exit before arriving at my mother's house, is a crucial turn to make, I can imagine what is waiting on me around the corner. It is about 8:30 p.m., and that means Betty should be almost high as a kike drinking with her misfit friends. The trees are so beautiful and big, leaning into the road as if asking to catch a ride. Long moss hanging from the tree limbs, like shadows of people. This is where I speed up, yet it is quite a steep curve.

Wow, I made it through, turning into mom's house. I find her at home with her drinking buddies, Boo-pep, Mike, and Freddie. She is always happy to see me, prefers to call me her pretty one or the bitch. Of course, I can be when she has had too much to drink. I become the bitch as soon as I find her liquor bottles and emptied them in the toilet, world war three just broke loose. The remainder of the visit, I am in and out. She curses when I come in, and when I leave, worse than a sailor, "that got damn bitch, keep fucking with my shit."
Sharon is nowhere to be found, Jennifer still at work, and Joyce went bogging for crabs in that funky muddy river. Guess I am on my own; granny is about five miles into the

city of Beaufort. A small colonial like area, tucked away behind some woods, cozy. Slavery time homes with the slave quarters in the backyard away from the main home. You get the idea, "master will meet me in the backyard later on tonight."

Pulling up to granny's, I notice Lonnie sitting on the steps sucking on a joint and looking as if he is one of whistler's son, steps unto the lawn, and opens the car door. What a sight for sore eyes, but he was happy to see me. Back pockets of his pants slapping together with each step he took; one wallet was stuffed more than the other. That is my uncle Lonnie. I remember him looking like Prince, singing like Prince, playing musical instruments like Prince, but now, he looks like the super on the PJs. He wears his hair part straight down the middle and combs down by his ears. That was cool in the 1960s, not now. All he does is look for someone to smoke weed with, and then he will always have something to smoke. A wife and seven children plus eight more by other women, and he thinks that he still got it going on...hot damn.

Uncle Lonnie has lived with granny most of his life, with the exception of the four years he was married. Safiya lives with granny as well; she is her eldest son, youngest daughter that suffered a closed head injury when she was nine days old. This happened in a car accident that killed her mother and wounded her other three siblings, but no one was as bad as Safiya's. Not able to do much other than clap her hands with sheer *enjoyment*. She does not receive visitors often, but it is a blast when my family comes to town or even just me.

I like to shoot the shit with Safiya, and she just lights up. She likes to tell granny what you are doing. She will cry out mama, mama, that is all she can say, but it is enough in how she announces mama. Granny knows you are into something you have no business being in. she has this ear to ear smile when I ask her if she has gotten a job, a man, or started to walk yet. I love her, she is dear to me, well, it is time to get ready, shower, touch up my hair, and slide into my sexy little black dress. Yah, baby, I am going to be the hottest shit in the club tonight. Very tasteful and elegant Versace dress, with Jimmy Cho 'Crown' Pump with Champagne glitter fabric and diamond accessories, fabulous as the happy gay guys say.

I think I should call up Diane, Darlene, Dessa, and Ellie; we went to nursing school together. Ellie dropped out and went a different direction with her education, a Jersey girl. The welfare, government cheese projects Jersey girl that got amnesia after marrying the airplane mechanic. Darlene was the mentally challenged one; everyone needs a friend, right? She was beautiful with makeup on, and would not put one foot outside the door without applying that casket ready to melt off make-up. Want to know why, she was the exact twin of her father, Mr. Smith, faceoff. Believe it or not, she married a man that looks just like Barney from Mayberry R.F.D, and the only difference is the dark skin tone. She was as senseless as a doorknob, but could pull a man, the dumb black blonde. Dessa was in the same shoes as Darlene, her wishful thinking ass. Wishing she looked just like Whitney Houston, my God. I just smiled; no words needed to come from my mouth on that one. She did have long, pretty hair — nothing in resemblance that I could recognize, was similarly close to Whitney.

I suggest that the ladies meet up with me at the Officer's Club on the Air-Station, and we could move on into the night from there. The natural, black beauty, with long lock's shimmering and silky bouncing back and forth on her rump; Flawless, smooth pecan tan skin, full lips that will give any man an erection as he passes by with just a glimpse. Men have stumbled and fallen from the mere sight of these lips. Hips stack high enough to serve up a cup of coffee without the slightest spill. The legs connected to those hips are succulent, could make a man mouth run water. Yet I was never vain or superficial, my friends took care of that area.

Back in the day, I dated a few Military men but chose not to marry anyone. I had pretty good taste in men, but sometimes their character was flawed. It was always something that stood out about the individual. For instance, Chuck, is a drill instructor from Parris Island, slim, muscular hard body, strong Ghanaian accent. Chuck appeared to be a rattlesnake, but he was sweet as a kitten, or at least I knew how to make him purr. We always had some type of hook-up, the girls and I. Chuck's drill buddy Drummond, became Darlene's lover. She fell deep for this guy. It is just something extra about a foreign man. Getting back to chuck, we spent time together for two years; he got out of the service and returned to New York. He had his mind set on something about wanting to be a cop, ha, ha, ha, a crooked cop was my take. He came to visit a few times during the year, until one year, he did not show up. But it could have been because I moved to Rochester New York with Joe and did not leave a forwarding address. During his visits, I met his brother Virgil; he was taken by how our relationship seemed genuine. Virgil said, "you have made an impact on my brother; he is calm, willing, almost submissive. I have never seen that side of him, ever." I think chuck was one man in my life that I loved him until he did the unspeakable, slept with the known town prostitute BIG LINDA, wow. Big Linda, was a Big woman, like Madea.

Then Bruce arrived, my Air Station man, wild man. He was in a fight every Friday or Saturday night. He was always fighting, known as the Mike Tyson, of the Air Station without the muscles, voice, or the punch. Bruce was interestingly a little younger. He could drink you under the table, beat your ass, and then became the rhythm less white boy. Bruce and I were an item for a minute, and then my eyes opened to the fact that he was holding one of Darlene's boob's in his hand and mine in the other while looking straight ahead. What was going on in her mind or his at the time, I don't know, but I wasn't blind. I don't drink alcohol nor did I smell it, so I was sober in every sense. I called up Frank. I watch that mother fucker Bruce for just a little while, and his ass was gone, but not before there was someone to replace his sorry ass. Now, what was funny, I met Frank at the Quarter Deck on the Navy Base on

Saturday night. He was intriguing, sexy lips, look like he could hold a clit down without coming up for air.

Frank and I *enjoyed* going to dinner, movies, strolls on the waterfront, sitting in the swings on the pier. Frank was a funny man; he was new to town, a new crop of Marines for Drill Instructor School from all over the United States. We talked and danced, and he asked me out to the movies. I declined because of Bruce, then that moment passed. Frank put my number in his jeans pocket for future use. So, thanks to my friend Darlene and my boy Bruce, I called up frank.

Frank arrived at my apartment at about five o'clock in the evening. Downtown Beaufort is still warm and sunny with a faint breeze brushing against your cheeks, made a nice time for another stroll on the waterfront. This is where you or everyone is seen with their man if they want to show him off. New meat in town, I got him first, or he is with her, I can pull him, shit. So, Bruce was at the apartment when frank arrived, no big deal to me. Frank did not come inside but did come up in the driveway. Yes, Bruce did not ask questions nor was an explanation given for Frank presence, no reason too. I stepped out of the apartment and asked Bruce to lock up when he left. You see, he got into another fight, this time, he was Evander with the ear bitten off, all taped up looking for sorrow and I had none to offer, and sorry mother fucker.

Frank and I met up at St. Regis for dinner before hitting the dance floor. Nice ride, a classic convertible Eldorado tan and mocha with a red man driving. Yes, lord, well, frank and I dated for three years, sometimes on and then sometimes off. He was a sweet rebel without a cause. He could not cook, but always gave me dinner and a smile. I came home from work, and he stopped me at the door, ran into the kitchen, and opened the oven door slowly. Of course, I was anticipating what he could have possibly cooked. There it was, my favorite item to eat, a payday candy bar on a plate. He just took it out of the oven. It was so thoughtful, and I gave him a big grin, and sex right on the stove, hot.

There is a knot at the door, and it is Bruce, frank invites him to come in and have a seat. His face is twisted with anger, but I don't understand why at this point. Out of nowhere, Bruce grabs Frank's shirt from the back and pulls him down to the floor. Shit no, we can't have that here. They rolled outside into the yard, and I stayed inside looking out the window. Bruce was about two inches taller than frank, but he did not seem to mind. It was an air station marine against a Paris Island marine. Frank was getting the best of Bruce, Bruce fell down to the ground after a hard punch to the face, crying like a bitch. Then the bite happened, and it was over. Frank is the man winning the brawl. After Bruce bit him on the ear, he started to throw punches left and right, faster and faster.
Air Station marines and Paris Island marines were always rivalling when it came to the local women. Frank went back to the base to clean up and will come back later on. Bruce still seeking sympathy and attention, which he got neither. Upon frank's return, we went to the drive-in movie theatre. I left Bruce on the steps and suggested that he call

Darlene. He looked at me with stupidity. That was that for
Bruce.

Frank stayed close to my side for three years, mostly joyful
and loving occasions, with the usual ups and downs in a
relationship. He had very warm ways of receiving me when
I came home from work. We like some of the same things,
but he was more adventurous than I. We would go for long
rides in the country, watch western movies, Shane's, old
yellow were his favorites, and the rifleman was mine. I
watched him cry through old yellow and laughed like a
cheesy cat. He was very affectionate, liked to touch, feel,
and sit close. Our love line was to say, "I love you too
much and some more," whenever he was leaving. We
visited my mother, and she was always on his case about
something. Visiting his parents in Virginia and his two ex-
girlfriends visiting him, at his mother's was a little
awkward. These witches visited every day until we were
ready to leave and drive back to South Carolina.

Those ex-girlfriends were vultures, even the fat one. She
told me, "I know what he likes, and it is not you- bones."
The other ex was his baby mama, and she could not return
to Maryland unless he took them home. I felt that if she had
to resort to this type of tactic, then so be it. I believe and
have learned that a man is going to do what a man wants to
do, and a woman will do the same as well.
Frank was focused on getting embassy duty and a tour
overseas. His future plans were about the military and not a
family. He did not say it right out, but I could hear it in his
voice. Our relationship took another turn, and our closeness

became distance a little more each day. To top this situation, that bitch Darlene interrupting again. Frank dropped Darlene off at her parents on his way to the base one particular night. Then he came over after running his PT the next morning. I had plans to go to Savannah, Georgia, for a little shopping, then Hilton Head Island, to see a few friends. After shopping for a while, I got tired and decided to put my bags in the back seat of the car. I found some makeup on the floor, as if they may have fallen out of a purse. Maybe that bitch even placed them there for me to intentionally fine.

I picked up the makeup and kept it, just to see if she or he was going to ask about the mask maker. Yet, I was waiting to see if this bold bitch was going to show up at my front door makeup-less, with her man face on. So, I waited in silence, not saying a word to either. Acting like I did not know a thing was going on. This bitch had the notion of telling me about another haggard face woman he was "messing with." As each day passed, I distanced myself more and more from Frank and Darlene. Putting them in the past, she approaches me as I was sitting on the swing. "You know Frank is dating one of my friends?" I said, "Really?" under my breath, and I was screaming you man looking mother fucking bitch, with a smile. She comes back saying, "Oh. I have a new boyfriend, and he is married. I want you to meet him. His name is Donald." well, I was not interested in meeting any of her boyfriends. Ellie was to come over later in the evening, for some girl talk. Darlene decides to stop by anyway, with her married man. This is the moment where my day became one of my best days.

This experience left a lasting impression on my mind. I had never seen a black man that looked like the identical twin of a white man. Okay, hold onto your britches, this Donald looked exactly like Bonnie from Mayberry RFD. You know Andy, Opie, and Mrs. Bea's Bonnie. I made a comparison of the resemblance, and her big bottom lip dropped, and Ellie's eyes popped. However, Donald replied, I get that a lot. Same face, same body type, same walk, scary. He eventually divorced and married Darlene, and they moved to North Carolina. After two to three years, she returned to Beaufort, divorced and on the prowl. Drive-by calls and lights blinking had turned back on her, some woman repeated what she had done to Bonnie's wife a few years earlier.

I did not see Dessa during this time; she was too busy plotting for her baby daddy to marry her before he died. She had plenty of time to work on this one, in addition to her crop of military men on the side. She was all about the flowers, candy, and hotel rooms. Oh girl, he got me some beautiful flowers, you need to see this. Shit, why do I need to see what your fucking boyfriends are giving you? I don't need that. It is for you. But I understand if no one is giving you something, then you are not putting out nor have time for that individual. If your rank was not master sergeant, gunny, or officer, no way was you getting old girl time. Her baby father was cool, owned his business, and did not

worship her butt-forehead ass. He knew she was a trailer
park gold-digging hoe.

Dessa fiancé raced motorcycles as a hobby. One evening he
was going too fast, lost control of his bike going around a
curve, and crashed around a light pole. Both of his legs
were broken, and he suffered massive internal injuries.
Going through the operation and during recovery, she
asked him to marry her. Oh my God, were my thoughts,
what the hell is she thinking. Of course, I knew this trailer
park hoe was trying to get an inheritance. Gold digger
trailer park hoe asked this man to marry her on his death
bed. His family was present and outraged that she showed
no concern other than for her own selfish needs. The family
was already against him being with her from the start.
He died within hours of being in the recovery room at the
hospital. She seemed to be okay with it, after learning that
her son would be getting a social security check and left
him a few acres of land and some money. She was such a
predator, worse than a blood-sucking leach when it came to
men. Every man in her mind that saw her wanted her. It
could have been ten women in a group, and the men would
pick only Dessa.

Then there was Hyme, the Panamanian marine, an older
man. He did not see her true color for years. But I
enlightened him after a while; it was payback time for this
bitch. The next victim was married, but his wife was in
another state, Atlanta, Georgia, as with a lot of marines.
The two were inseparable, yet she saw many others. I will
let her rest for a while and introduce you to Diane. I think

she was a friend, more than the other things. While in College, Diane moved in with me for a year. She was dating Bunting, from Philly. Paris Island marine and a very loose man married with children and other women as well. Philly and Diane was an item, and this man slanged dick like it was a roping contest.

This man had an outrageous sexual appetite, married, and carried on in a relationship with Diane for years and multiple abortions. King of the roller coaster rides Philly divorced his wife, and married Diane. When Diane and Dessa married their cheating boyfriends, I guess they did not think that one day, the Karmic tables will also turn on them. Now, as the wives, they are also being cheated on and wondering why is he cheating on me, shit you did the same thing to get him, remember? After Diane and Philly were married, they relocated to North Carolina as his new duty station and of course, fresh meat. They had a daughter as husband and wife, but about 12 abortions as boyfriend and girlfriend, wow. When the bliss was over, they returned to his old stomping grounds, Beaufort. It all fell apart, Diane was alone, angry, and fat. Abortions do make you blow up, especially after a dozen.

Anyway, she was a totally different person when she returned home. She was not as friendly or inviting. I went to visit her at her home on one of my visits to see my grandmother. Her presence was dull, and I felt unwelcomed, which was probably true. I shook it off and tried to be nice about it, making short conversations. This mullet face, mosquito looking bitch, was snobbish and sad.

Oh well, that is life in a nutshell, grin and bear it, and move on. I returned to Atlanta, called her a few times, but she never returned my calls. I was thinking, "Shit," she ate my food and slept in my apartment, farted, and shitted in my bathroom. I helped her out in her time of need. Okay, I made a decision; I decided to look at things in a different light. Maybe, she felt our friendship was from a different time in her life. Yes, I can agree with that, so with that thought, I saw it as we grew apart because I was happy without her as a friend.

When this batch of girlfriends was no longer part of my life, I did not make friends with females, just males. Males are much easier to deal with, not so much damn drama. I was no longer listening to how super stupid I was, because of how I was treated by my man.

Life can be much harder than anyone expects, and a Prayer even if it is in your own words can be so soothing like a "good cry."

Blessed am I, blessed am I
In the sweetness Of the Lord's eyes
Blessed am I That can see the divine
Leading me at this point in time
Blessed am I That the Lord
Has me in his favor
He is my Lord and Savior
Blessed am I to bend my knees
In prayer to rise to a new start
Each day, My Lord

Makes a way
Blessed am I
Blessed am I
In the purest
Of heart, praising
My Lord in his Great Glory
Blessed am I

I strongly believe that somehow, we get exactly what we need, even if we don't recognize it at the moment.

The Beauty of my Spirit In my mind eyes, is this what I see?
The beauty of my spirit Serene, amiable, and devout
Holding me together as a shore by the sea
Loyal, warm, efficient and caringly
The beauty of my spirit A perfect whole
Content with what I see spiritually, protective and motherly
The beauty of my spirit a reflection of life
Dreams and no sorrow yet a part of me
Cooperative and loving diligently
Where rest may not go
But the beauty of peace follows
I will soothe in the beauty of my spirit
That loves me
Focused on
Being kind, positive and upbeat
With high integrity

It is beautiful when you can see this in someone else

This Life
Grand as it may be, it is not free
Even though it was given
To you and me to live abundantly
You pay with loss and grief Mostly Love that you see
This life Planned by a higher One
Is not for us to suffer and fight
With all our might
This life yet
Sacred and sweet
A time to learn
To keep our soul safe and free
During hours of darkness
This will not pass by me
This life although
Can be more
It is not what you get
Down this dirt road
It is how you made your way
In clearness or haze this life
I heard from an old soul that our life is our plan, then our
reward is his glory.
Does he not see my ways and count my every step?

A Painful Exit

The vision I see in my head
Brings tears to my eyes as I stare
At the vivid screen in my memory
A painful exit is what I see
I gave my eye upon her lifeless body
Holding her hands and whispering softly
I love you, and I understand you are ready to go
Pass on
To a Better place
I know a painful exit this must be
For the child within me
Squeeze my hand if you understand
And I will let you
Go
I will let you
Go

On this day, I am at my mother's bedside, she asks for a drink of water, she asks to go to the restroom, anything to get the oxygen mask off her face. I said to my mother, "stop it, I know what you are doing, and she smiled her last smile."

A painful exit for me
Lord this is what I see
Lying flat on her back
Eyes bulged and jelled
From electrical shock
That was supposed to

Bring back life-but failed
A painful exit this will be
Her eyes taped shut
As I stand by her bed
As I hold her hand
Comfort is a must and time is near
I really don't want her to leave
In prayer, I plead
A painful exit this will be
Lord helps me to set her free
I know she must go
It is time to tread no more
On the wandering grounds
Her life has seen
A painful exit it will be

I never thought that my mother would leave this earth so soon- I was so hurt and angry.

In a Moment
Sharing a beautiful moment with her
As she slowly fades
Only God knows I'll be lonely
For the rest of my days
A painful exit is what I see
Her spirit responds in a positive way
To the loving things I had to say
I only wish that she made her way
To a better existence than today
A painful exit is what I see
My mother unresponsive
To me
Her hand casing mine
Full with love and uncertainty
I know my mother's eyes
Another day I will see

It took me so long to reach this place in my heart, yet, it is still filled with tears. In my mother's children and their children, I still see her and hear her voice.

One generation will commend your works to another; they will tell of your mighty acts.

I trust in You. O Lord, I say. " You are my God." My times are in your hands.

Quiet Moments of another Day
I will take a quiet moment to reflect on another day
Being at peace within myself
Catching one instance in time to see beyond
My humble ways- embracing appreciation
For what I will leave behind
I will take a quiet moment to reflect
The serenity of another day
In this time
I will reflect on the intensity given to those
Whom I diligently cared for
In such an efficient way
I will take a quiet moment to reflect on another day
With consciousness in mind
Sincere in thought, a beautiful spirit is about to depart
Sallying forth on a new passage with the Purest of heart
Sharing the beginning of another day
To reflect on quiet moments
Outpouring in stillness from the core of my heart
Quiet moments of another day
I will reflect
Life is such a journey that we sometimes forget the beauty that can be found in having a few quiet moments to ourselves.

In quietness and in confidence shall be your strength

I Knew Love
I knew love by the feeling in my heart
Warmth from head to toe spreading forth
Overcome by a feeling of ease and joy
As my body glide to his knees
I sat tearfully on the floor
I knew love by the Feelings in my heart
As he pulls away ripping the threads that twine
His heart with mine
I could not let him go- my heart pounder in pain
I begged him to stay
Not leaving me in arrears
I hung onto his robe for all there might be
I cried don't go Please stay with me
I knew love was struggling
To getaway
I could not set him free
Whatever you ask for in prayer, believe that you have received it, and it will be yours. I am still asking.

Embracing Hearts
Entering together as one
Sharing divine love that entwines
Our hearts we will never be apart
We are embracing hearts with
Permeating thuds from afar
You and I Love Forevermore
joined as ONE
We will embark on this journey
Engulfed in God's grace
Embracing Hearts
Until our ending days
The finest thing in life
Our Love
Is to be Blessed twice
I found you, and you found me
We have found
The essence in LIFE
In the Lord's eyes, there is no longer an empty dwelling
Of a sacrifice
You are here with me
Now and forevermore
Embracing hearts
As One
With the Lord as our Guiding light
We will never be apart

I have Rejoice in all the good things my God has given to me, and I have wallowed in misery and rejection, just realizing it was his protection.
The Agile One

Illuminating in the light
Opening the hearts
Of many souls
Genuine, humble, tranquil
Agile one stands
By his throne
Keeping his RIGHT hand in mine
As we move on
Yet near to the light
Sorrow comes to none
The Agile One
Is not alone
Standing at his throne
"HERE"
The Agile One
With hopes of splendor
Intense focus interweaving together
Hearts forever confidently, without doubt
Opening the window of your soul
The Agile One
"THERE"
He sees an
Entity glancing, eyes shining bright
Warranted it is not night
The Agile One
A perfect Whole

Content with what he sees
A reflection of life
That puts him on
Bending knees
The Agile One

Thanks, be unto God for His unspeakable gift

Doc

Shasha hums and moans and it turns her on to see him lift up off the pillow as she strokes his oily dick. Her pussy cat is so wet and ready. It is pulsating, wanting him to fuck her over and over again. It was one of the most euphoric joyful experiences. Doc was happy and I was happy enough for the both of us…we rolled over and took a nap. We woke up, ate bananas; Doc satisfies the pulsating pussy cat and goes to work, leaving Shasha with only the memories of shared pleasure for twelve hours. Doc had a long night at work and could wait to return home to his Babe…Shasha. He was contemplating in his mind all the pleasure they shared before he went to work and forward thinking about where he wanted to start all over again. To his surprise Shasha had to leave but she left some pussy juice in a specific spot on his pillow with a note.

"Good Morning Doc, how are you on this wonderful Wednesday morning. I hope you didn't get enough of me last night because I am still craving you. I am in class; but I left you a smell and you can lick and suck later. We can text if you want to chat. Well, I want to dirty chat."

Not getting much rest for the past seven days Doc was feeling a little under the weather but always used reverse psychology and it paid off. Doc, I am so sorry I drained you to the point you are feeling awful, but you need some rest and fluids. Wishing I lived closer, I could come over, and you rest your head in my lap. Babe, try Tylenol Sinus blue or yellow color, and not in combination with other cold medicines. I will check on you later.

Darling Sweet Doc called, and Shasha knew she had to go comfort him. She could hear in his voice that he needed at least a warm, soothing hug, something to ease his mind. Shasha planned to spend at least two days with her heart's desire. So, she called ahead and made reservations at their spot at the Hilton Garden Suites. She only told Doc, "I am coming." In a matter of hours, she was on the road, driving, singing, and happy that she will be in his arms again. Yet, sad for what he is going through at the moment. She decides not to call him until after checking into the Hilton. During the entire drive, Shasha was picturing what she could do to lift his spirits. Maybe, what he needs is only to have someone to feel close to, whatever, Doc needed from her, she was willing to fulfill his needs. Shasha called Doc and gave him the room number and he assured her that he would be there within the hour. He put her on speaker as he packed his bag.

Shasha wanted to know if Doc remembered how they met. He asked her to tell him the story. Well, I like how we met and that I was so forward, out of my usual element, thanks for answering all my questions. I like hearing your voice every day. I like your text messages and being your Sunshine in the morning, and at night, I like that you offered to rub my feet, give me a massage, and take off my shoes and a hundred other things you do. I appreciate you. Within the hour Doc arrives to the Hotel, Shasha is looking out the window to see when his SUV roles up and he steps out with is overnight bag. She knew he would feel better once she relaxed him.

He came in and sat in this blue arm rest chair, very comfortable chair she took off his shoes got on her knees and gave him a long kiss and hug. Baby, you are working too hard and not getting enough rest. So, I don't want you to do anything but move from this chair to the bed on my command. He wanted to freshen up and Shasha was game for that as she was about to make him her strawberry tootsie roll lollipop for about 30 minutes. She motioned to pull him from the chair so he can lay down in the bed. She rubbed his legs from his hips to his feet and wrapped each in hot towels. It was so good he felt he should be paying her for all the attention and pampering. They enjoyed each other company and she got on top of Doc and fell asleep as he embraced her in his arms. She knows when he needs only rest, so he rested for the next day.

Shasha asks Doc to help her drive her car from Charleston to Atlanta. They head out driving with relaxing clothing on… Doc, just a shirt and shorts. Doc starts out driving at night and Shasha is sleeping when Doc reaches over and caresses Shasha thighs, she lays her seat back as Doc rubs her hot juicy pussy, he then sticks his fingers inside her and starts to fingerfuck her, caressing her clit and lips then he pulls his finger out and tastes Shasha juice then rubs it on her breast as her nipples get hard. Shasha then reaches over and starts to stroke Docs cock. She then bends over and puts it in her mouth, giving Doc head as he is driving down the highway. Doc continues to finger Shasha as she moans and sucks faster and harder as Doc strokes faster and deeper. They pull into the rest area, and park, Shasha climbs into the backseat. After that stimulating rest stop, we were back on the road and a little thirsty and wet. We stop at a store off the next exit and get some water and a wipe down then headed out to Atlanta. It was a turnaround trip, so I took care of business and we went back to Charleston. He was still off but I had to return to work the next morning at 8 a.m. it was an oral night so I could get some rest because once he got started there was no stopping. No amount of music was going to keep me awake for a 5-hour drive. So, he was kind and thoughtful and served me up. I left at 5:30 a.m. and could not make it into work so I took leave for the day. Doc was constantly on my mind. We exchange text messages. Good Morning Sunshine (his nickname for Shasha) Headed to work. I am still fighting this cold. Have a Fantastic day and week?

Shasha would text back…Good Morning Babe, how are you? But there was not much conversation during the day, because Doc works nightshift 12 hours and officiates games for 3-4 hours and coach's basketball. Shasha, was a straight 8-hour shift Monday-Friday. She made a trip two to three times a month for two to three days and he was always available. There daily morning and night text messages between visits was refreshing each looked forward to the nice and nasty messages coming down the pipe line. Shasha really enjoyed the dirty talk as they video chat and she watched his dick grow. He did not believe in masturbating but she did. Shasha, made a video of her voice cumin and sent it to Doc, as an eye opener along with a text message…Good Night my visual stimulation, I am going to bed. Long distance does require more of an effort. Things were going good or so Shasha thought. She called Doc, texted Doc, and no response. You said we would be together, and then you said, you will let me know, come on now, be fair and equal. You know that's no way to treat the heart you hold. Okay, he has a lot of shit on his mind, well, so do I and he is my escape, but I will give him this one. About a month goes by and the trips decrease, texts messages slow down, and phone calls so Shasha realizes something else has his attention. No forcing the issue but Shasha is in Charleston for a business trip when Hurricane Matthew stirs up. Shasha flight is canceled, and she is unable to leave town. She calls Doc, who is trying to leave town. He diverts from leaving and picks up Shasha. The roads are closed. They pick up some supplies and head to Doc's place. The storm picks up. They showered and are sitting around when they lose power. Forget about the last 30 days just stay in the here and now. They light some candles and have a snack and drinks. The storm gets stronger with loud thunder and lightning. Shasha comes closer to Doc as she is frightened. Doc asks for a kiss Shasha says no then whispers in Doc ear. "Take It" Doc kisses her luscious lips then sticks his tongue deep in her mouth and pulls her closer then grabs her ass cheek as Shasha lets out a moan, he then grabs both cheeks and rubs them. Doc kisses her neck and down to her breast. He bites her nipples as she moans with pleasure.

Doc kisses her stomach and her navel. He then lays her down as he removes her clothes. Doc kisses her hot juicy pussy. He sticks his tongue inside her as she screams out Doc, Doc, oh Doc, Babe. Doc sucks and licks her as she tries to pull away. He pulls her closer and sucks all her juice as she screams and releases her hot juicy cum. Shasha then climbs on top and slides his hard cock deep inside her creamy wet pussy. She strokes him for a while, then turns around and rides his cock reverse cowgirl style. Doc grabs her ass and smacks it. Shasha strokes harder with each smack. Shasha turns around, and Doc fondles her breast squeezing her nipples.

They roll over in bed, and Doc gets on top and put Shasha legs on his shoulders and strokes her. Shasha is moaning and begging for it all. Fuck me, and she calls out. Doc goes harder and harder. They are both sweating. Shasha lets out a loud scream and releases her hot creamy cum all over Doc's cock. Shasha then says, let me taste you. Shasha pulls out, and Shasha puts Doc cock in her mouth then sucks his balls. She strokes his cock in her mouth, taking it all down the back of her throat. She sits on the bed as he stands in from of her, gently guiding her head to the depth that was most pleasurable, taking it all in her mouth over and over again, not letting the suction break, sucking and licking like candy until Doc lets out a loud scream. "Oh Shasha," as he burst in her mouth. Shasha sucks harder taking all of Doc juice in her mouth, not wasting a drop she wipes the corners of her lips. Tasty, she *enjoyed* it more than he did. Shasha gets out of the bed, tells Doc not to move. She goes to the bathroom and clean up the excess fluids and brings him a steaming hot towel. The soothing warm towel after such an amazing fuck was so relaxing. Shasha took the warm towel and wrapped it around Doc's cock for a few seconds, she bathes his cock until the warmth was gone, she got a dry towel and patted his cock and balls dry, and she gave it one last hard suck, and they took a nap as the storm continues. They make love for another two days until the storm left. Shasha returned to Atlanta feeling good but bruised. She reached out to him a little less frequently, guess the Honeymoon phases was over.

A Few Days Later

Shasha is in Charleston for union training and is sightseeing downtown when she hears her name being called. She turns around and is quite surprised to see Doc with this big smile on his face. They hugged, and Shasha drops her purse. They bend down to pick it up, and they are face to face, so Doc gives her a big kiss sticking his tongue in her mouth. She says she has to go back to training. Later, in the back of her mind that silent dialogue is back. "Girl you know you have to stop this shit right here. That other side of the Gemini, was coming forward. Training ended late and the social last past 10 p.m. and I tired. Around 8a.m. I got a text message from Doc, it read…

Good Morning Sunshine, but I did not respond right back as I normally do but my intention was by the time class ended. Shasha goes to Walmart after training where she'd purchased some cosmetics products and then heads back to the hotel. She arrives in her room, and to her surprise, Doc is in bed waiting for her. She made a habit of leaving a key for him at the desk, just in case she was late arriving. Shasha showers after a long day of training. Afterwards, she asks Doc to rub her body with the baby oil she just bought. Doc rubs her neck then her back down to her thighs, Shasha stops Doc as she says the Massage is making her extremely hot. Doc stops and then starts to kiss Shasha's soft, luscious lips, and then he kisses her neck and ears down to her soft breast and gently bites her nipples. He always knew just the right amount of pain to mix with the pleasure. Doc proceeds down her stomach until he stops at her hot juicy pretty pink pie. There he kisses, sucks, and licks it until Shasha starts to moan gently. Doc continues as the moans become louder. Doc licks Shasha's hot spot making her sweat until she tried to hold his head back to no avail. Shasha likes to revisit the day they met and Doc loves hearing the story.

Shasha's account of what happened on 10/25/2016, meeting Doc. My group and I arrived at the Hilton Garden around 3:00 p.m. on 10/25/2016. As we were getting out of the Van, Adam asked, "is it okay if my brother Doc meets us for lunch?" I replied, "yes, is he married?" Adam laughed. We entered the Hotel lobby entrance, and I walked up to the desk to check the four of us in. I was a little anxious to meet his big brother, Doc. We decided where we were going for lunch; rather, it would be Chilies, Caribous, or Outback. Outback, it was. However, I was not hungry for food but had a taste for something sensational. The body knows what it wants even before setting eyes on it.

It was as if I was a lioness, laying and waiting for my king to show, from around a big bush. I pictured him as being strong, tall, and handsome with a dark completion. Yeah, boy, I was wishing some of it measured up. We put our luggage in our rooms and drove to the restaurant, which was only about two minutes away. As we sat at the table to have lunch, Adam announced that his brother was just a few minutes away and should arrive soon. We ordered drinks and appetizers and our main course. I ordered clam chowder soup and a Caesar salad with a raspberry ice tea. Eating my soup, my head was down, but I heard Adam say, "Hey, what's up bro?" My eyes peeled upwards. Standing across the other side of the table in front of me was Mr. Doc. Silently, in my thoughts, as I was thinking to myself, my God, he is big and tall… 7'6" I could get lost in those arms; I would love to get lost in those arms. He had a sweetness about him that was a little shy, but I could just slop him up like biscuits and gravy. So, I just smiled for a few minutes, hoping he did not recognize the type of smile I was giving him. If I was in his place, the quest, I would know that smile miles away.

For some reason, not sure which one yet, I felt a sense of I know you, and I want you all at once. Now, the drilling starts. "Well, Doc, you are Adams's 'big" brother?" His reply was, "yes, I am, and you are?" Eager, no, I was eager and answered with a smile as I lick my top lip, "Shasha." I love the way my name sounded even when I pronounced it seductively. Doc gave a smile that was warming to my body from across the table. All the heat rushed to the area of my pussy. It was as if I just sat in something so soothing and moist, like a set of lips and a tongue. I am glad he could not see under the table. I was having a fight with my pussy trying to signal this man. Hey mister, the pussy under the table hasn't seen or touched a dick in ten years. Your warmth and touch are needed. Doc had no idea what the pussy had in mind for him. As the questioning moves further along, I got a more definite yes answer; he was forthcoming. I asked and told him I wanted to know everything from A to Z. He was a willing participant, answered all questions without hesitation. Right off, I loved his height, damn no more 5'2, 7'6" has arrived. Did wonder if the dick would be too big.

Oct 2017

Charleston for one week at the Hilton Garden Inn. I tried to get the same room as to share with Doc in Oct 2016, but it was already occupied. I asked Dena to just place me on that side of the hall, and things would work out just fine. I came to town three days earlier than the training was to start just to spend some uninterrupted time with Doc. I just wanted to give him all of me and feel all of his fire deep inside penetrating my walls, all of his loving I have been longing for.

I did not see Doc in November or December, partly due to a few things my eye locked in on during the second October visit. If shit was just coming out, if God was at work in this because I asked for signs to determine if he was genuinely into me or just faking the funk. After the coffee cup with the red lipstick was taken out of the dishwasher, and I was given coffee. I felt some kind of way. What the fuck, this must have been intentional; no way, this was a mistake. God was really making it retardedly clear as I asked.

While standing at the stove preparing the coffee, Doc asked, "Shasha, would you like a full or half of cup." She replied half due to the lipstick on the inside as well. Doc, she replied, I will add the cream and sugar, and I would prefer to have hazelnut. He walked over to the stool she was sitting on and placed the cup of coffee in front of her. Shasha, sat there on her stool, pondering how to present the lipstick and coffee issue to Doc as he sat across from her reading his newspaper. All was quiet, Shasha called out Doc's name, and he answered in his low sexy monotone voice, "yes baby."

By chance, did you see the lipstick on this cup that has the coffee in it that I am about to drink? His concerned reply was no, what do you mean, she showed him the lipstick after wiping the area clean with a moist towelette as she explained how greasy lipstick and dishwashing don't work. Oh, you must be mistaken, so she passed him the tissue. He glances at the towelette and put the newspaper up to his face. The sharpness that went through her body only lasted a few minutes, but leaving was the initial thought. But she stayed and told him she understood, and he was helping her more than he knew.

Under her breathe, there was a dialogue of motherfuckers, son of a bitch, all while smiling and having a conversation.
A few hours passed, and they took a nap, after all, she promised to cook him dinner for the three days, she was going to be with him. Besides, she is married, just not happy, and no sexual contact with her husband other than titty sucking and pussy eating for a long, long, long period of time, shit for hours. So, she could not be mad as he said before he is human and a man. Is he supposed just to wait? She was thinking silently 'HELL YEAH," but responded: I understand, and I love you. Her eyes were fire red with anger, and he saw that her words did not match the feelings on her face.

She climbed on top and gave him a passionate kiss, thinking this is going to end soon, but she did not want it to. Things kept showing up or became clearer and more obvious as the day went by and night rolled in., he went to officiate a game for a few hours but would return earlier than the night before which would be roughly 8 p.m. Shasha, went to the grocery store to buy what she was going to prepare him for dinner on night two. She bought steaks, white potatoes, corn on the cob, beer, and wine. She pan-seared the steak with onions, green peppers, and mushrooms and made a delicious brown sauce to drizzle over the loaded baked potato. The corn on the cob was sweet and juicy, after steaming and a little grilling just to give it a slight charcoal taste and add a little color.

Dinner was ready right at 7:45 p.m. she timed it perfectly as she was expecting him to arrive around 8 p.m. there is some noise at the door, as the key turns and the door opens, she sees this big ass smile like, honey I am home. She smiles back at him, and he said, damn it smells good in here, somebody might need to move to Charleston. He walks over to the counter and gives her a kiss on the forehead, washes his hands, and sits on the stool waiting to be served up.

Shasha prepares his plate and sets it in front of him. Doc asked what would he like to drink, and gave him a cold beer she had chilling on ice. After he was finished with dinner, they baked a pound cake together, but it did not turn out good, but she never told him why. It tasted like cake and looked like cake but did not rise up like a cake. She told him to add an ingredient that was not on the list, thinking it would work with the type of flour they were using, and it did not.

Mind you not, the refrigerator was packed with all sorts of prepared dishes, but damned again, because he is a single man with no time for a committed relationship, according to him. Yet what we shared was not just about sex, so he said, and I believed. I knew it was not only about the sex for me, but I felt so alive with him and making love to him felt like I was getting a refill of love and warmth and positive energy to lift me up off my feet from my Twin-flame. I love how his body moves on top of mine; everything we did together was a song, nothing but making sweeter music.

What I did to me so early in the morning

Between Us

While sitting at my desk doing my due diligence to complete some time-consuming work, I heard Adam asking, calling out Shasha to come outside. Come get some fresh air. I was so busy, responding to an outrageous email, I was still holding my pee since 09:00, and now it is 11:30. I was determined to finish my work before moving.

Another knock at the door, I got up to unlock the door and walked into the hall. Only to see what the employee wanted to talk about, and it was taking to long for him to get his point across. It was a personal issue that would require more time than I had available at the moment. As I was standing in the hall talking with an employee, I noticed Susie-q walking in with her camera phone, Adam was behind her smiling and Joyce behind him, oh my God. I see the top of the head of a tall man with glasses that had black and red rims. I knew those glasses, the eyes, and the face.
He was wearing a seductive grin and gave me the "hello, how are you" in the voice that melts my heart to my soul on another realm. I was not expecting him, and we had not spoken, only short, simple text messages with little meaning, good night Sunshine, good night Doc, good morning Sunshine, good morning Doc, have an awesome day, the string affect. I always had more to say but decided against it. I felt he was not in the same space as me with his feelings about us being together.

I was so happy to see him, so happy indeed that my body started to react as he walked closer, with that sweet smile. I had no idea how long he was going to be in town, but I was hoping it was at least for the night. We all walked into the office, and he sat at the table, looked up at me as I passed by to have a seat. We smiled at each other across the table; as his brother told him to come on, let's go the cafeteria to get some chicken. I asked, would you like to go with me out to lunch at my favorite restaurant. It's after two o'clock, and I haven't had breakfast or lunch. His reply was, "yes, of course." I went to the restroom to freshen up before our departure. I suggested that we take his vehicle instead of mine due to his long legs.

Bye, bye Adam, as we headed to the restaurant, I asked Doc what brought him to Atlanta. His reply was, I went to take care of a few things for my son and decided to stop by. I smiled, because his stopping by was more than three hours out of his way. We sat side by side at his request, and I asked him to tell me what's going on with him, what's new? He indicated there was nothing new, you know me, the same old thing, work, kids and work, doing what I have to do. Well, good to hear that too much has not changed since I last saw you. How about you? Wow, he said, let me see that, what? The ring, man, the old boy, went way out, two pieces. I smiled and told him you are still funny, stop it.

The waitress came back to the table and asked if we were ready to order. I only had lobster and shrimp brisk soup, and he had the grilled shrimp. Both of us had an Arnold

Palmer and ate a little bread and butter. He did butter my bread.

I was feeling warm, but the restaurant was really cold. All he had to do was hold me with one finger, and my body would heat up like a kittle blowing and whistling releasing the steam. I am sure he had no idea how his being so close was affecting me. I played it cool and continue to ask him questions about his visit.

"So, Doc, what time are you leaving?" Doc stated, "I am not sure, I am a little tired." I was thinking, sure you are tired. But in actuality, I am sure he was due for his hectic work schedule and the hours of driving. Are you going to your brothers, not sure yet? But he asks … are you free? I stated I could be. If you are tired, I could get you a room at the Hotel down the street off of Clairmont Road. I had a friend that stayed, and he indicated it was nice and cozy. I called to check on availability while we were still having a late lunch. There was a Hilton a few miles from my job that had availability, so I reserved it and gave him my card and ID so he could go get some rest. He dropped me off in front of the building, and I went back to work.

I thought my baby came to get him some good loving made a detour. I was ready to receive it all and make him climb the walls. But I had this other issue I had to take care of my husband's home first. So, I sent a text message regarding a special call meeting face to face, and I would be too tired to drive to his house, so I was going home. The situation I was currently in was not working out as I thought it would. I like the man I married, but I am not in love with him. I am in love with Doc, does he love me, and the jury is still out on that one. But who knows, yes, I know who knows. So, I pray for Doc to be in love with me and be my exclusive. I believe prayers come true, and there is something about him that keeps me connected and longing for him every day and every night. Shit, I wonder at times myself, what the hell is going on here. I see him when I close my eye, and I am not even sleeping. I have had this image in my head for many years, his body, standing in front of me, lying next to me in bed, but I never can see his face.

I put it to past life experience that would never should up, but it has manifested. I just can't let it go. I have tried, and when I think he is gone and make a move to prepare myself for days without him in my life, he shows up like magic. All he has to do is say I am missing you, and I would ask him, "When are you off? Tuesday, Wednesday, and Thursday." I am on the road on Tuesday morning and gone for the next three days.

It's not just the sex, it more and I can't explain it right now, but I am sure it could be explained by the time I am finished. It feels so good being in his presence, lying in his arms, kissing his lips, nibbling on his nipples, kissing his special spot that I just have to have. He gives me all that I need and wants, and I get it all without asking.

So, a few hours go by so fast. I needed to get a few items from the store for work the next day. I was spending the night with the man that I was in love with. I got in my car, and it is now about 7:00 p.m. I wasted time. I got a cute jeans dress and some personal hygiene items for the night. I arrived in room 333 at 7:30 p.m. Doc met me downstairs and we went to get him something to eat. It only took a few minutes, and he helped me bring my items upstairs. He had relaxed and read the newspaper, USA Today. He suggested that I take my shower, and I suggested that he go first, which he did. I wanted to take a relaxing hot tub bath. You know, to heat the pussy cat up even more. I took about 20 minutes, rinsed off, and wrapped a towel over my head and one around my body after drying off. A common thing for me to do, since the beginning, anytime when he was around, it was coming off anyway.

He said, "Baby is you okay?" and I said, "Baby, are you?" We talked for a little while, looked into each other's eyes. I was wondering, why does it have to be like this? I crave him and his touch — my body grievers when he runs his finger up and down my arm. I don't think he realizes what he does to me. I am thinking at the moment, get a grip girl. He is coming closer and closer and pops a kiss on my arm. I feel him kissing me all over, and the towels have disappeared. I missed the moment they fell off my body, and I was so much into what he had me feeling at the time. He is magic in every sense for me, and he brings me to a peak of feeling alive I have never experienced, I am completely awake, and my only desire is more. He takes me to a place that I often long to be when he is gone. I love to hear him say, Oh Baby, what are you doing to me? His questions guide me to please him in the manner he desires. I deliver what I feel he wants from me just when he needs it. It may seem calculated, but it is pure instincts. I know when to move, how to move, how long to stay, and when he will take over. We are so in the sink, and it is mind bothering.

We make passionate love for hours, switching back and forth with no regard as to who is taking control. I climb on top and ease his hard cock into my sweltering pussy, all I could hear was oooh shit. I ride like he is my Stallone clamping my legs tightly to the outside of his thighs. He lifts up his thighs, and I place my feet under his thighs for a firm grip and a must better ride. He holds my ass and helps to make it more forcefully, and I sigh and moan with the pleasure of feeling him deep inside me, and as I rise and the head is right at the entrance, what a big head you have, my dear, and we laugh.

I let down easy and lay on his stomach. The feeling is intensifying, and I am shaking as I lay my head on his chest just for a few seconds until the quake passes. He said, "Come on baby, get your dick."

Between us, we kiss and hug while I am still sitting on my Stallone. I don't want him to feel like he is not satisfied. It is with a mission that I take care of my man's needs to the fullest. I feel it; I do feel it like it is the first time. All I wanted was to feel like he wants me and needs me. He pulls that off effortlessly like we were made for one another. I yearn for him, to kiss his dick, just to have him rest his dick on my lips. I am more turned on than he is, sorry Babe. I feel that he wants the same as I do, so I give him all that I would want in return, and it works for us. He always says I am here, I have not changed, and I am still here. We roll, hug, kiss, and make love for hours rest sometimes and repeat always. I am on top, he is on top, he is between my legs I am between his legs, I am stroking him, and he is licking and sucking me. Oh, he lets me ride like I am a cowgirl, and I know what I am doing because I am giving him all of what he needs.

On my way

Doc texts me, he is missing me, it's Sunday, and he is off Tuesday morning Wednesday and Thursday. I told him I would be there Wednesday, but I change my mind and leave Tuesday morning and arrive around 1400 Tuesday afternoon. I call him once I am outside his apartment door. What are you doing? He responds with resting, and I say that's a good idea. Where are you, he asks, and I said outside your door, your neighbor let me in the gate. I met her on my last visit.

He opens the door, lets me in, and lands a hot kiss and hug on me as if he really missed me. I know he did.
My mind is on loving him for the next two days. We stop in the kitchen, and he wanted to clean, no baby, I have something for you. It isn't necessary to clean two plates right now. Come get your loving, and we move to the bedroom where I use the bathroom and freshen up after the 5 hours ride. Its 2:30 p.m. and he has to go to work at 4:00 p.m. and should be back around 9:00 p.m. he has to officiate a Volley ball game. He asks if I wanted to go with him to the game or stay and study. I chose to study and cook him dinner by the time he returns. I asked Doc what he would like for dinner, he wanted lima beans and I asked big beans or little he did not mind which one so I decided on baby lima beans, he wanted rice and fried chicken. I asked which part of the chicken, and he wanted legs and thighs. I went to the store as he was leaving for the game. We shared a few hot moments; no, we shared a long hot moment with 15 minutes to spare. I served him up with a

lot of kisses as in all over and a special hand massage with a specific twist that he adores feeling. I am doing that thing that he likes for me to do with my lips, and I love to see him lift up off the pillow and hear him say, "Damn baby, what are you doing to me." When I was finished, I told him that it is called "beat the clock." You get finished just in time to get where you are supposed to be.

We leave, and I put the directions for the store in my GPS. A one-mile drive down the road and I get all the items I need to prepare an awesome dinner for my man. I make it back to the apartment and get out the pots and pans. I am a little nervous because this isn't my first-time cooking dinner for him, but I want it to be perfect. Shit, I already told him my cooking is better than my lovemaking; he will be licking all ten. Now I have to prove I am right, making love to him and cooking a meal for him will be like I satisfied his heart and his soul equally yoked. I prepared everything perfectly, and just in time, dinner would still be hot. Did the lima beans with Ox tails, prepared the chicken and fried it in his mother's cast iron frying pan, of course. I thanked Ms. Jimmy for the use of her frying pan. He did not ask for Mac and cheese, but I baked a pan anyway, can't have all that and no mac/cheese. I got him a few Heinekens to go along with his dinner, something cold and refreshing before I got started on him. Everything was done by 8:40, and he arrived at 9:00 p.m. He opened the door to his apartment and said dam it feels good in here. I smiled, he gives me my favorite forehead kiss and heads to the bathroom. When he returned, he fixes his plate and I watched him *enjoy* his fourth meal that I prepared with so much love. He did not even add salt or pepper just kept saying how good everything tasted. I felt genuinely satisfied that I had made it, by giving his stomach something it needed first, ok, second. He is the sweetest thing to me, so gentle, caring, and loving. He sits on the chair, admiring me and saying, "Baby, that was a great meal; you might have to transfer to Charleston VAMC." I smiled as I sipped on my mini bottle of wine. Doc cleaned the kitchen after putting the leftovers up, and I sat and watched him. Wow, helpful too. He indicated that he needs about 20 minutes before he could take a shower, so he went and lay on the bed. I already had my shower, did not want to smell like chicken when he came home. I asked for one of his t-shirts since all I had on was a towel, and he was too tired and full at the moment to take advantage of me like I wanted him to. So, I watched TV while he napped.

Second's NO NAP (LOL) Doc wants Shasha to climb on board his soul train and go for a long ride...she was willing but not able. Shasha told Doc "baby, this leg is not going to make it. How about I give you a little lick, lick, lick." Doc, so sweet and thoughtful, did not want her to do too much work. He felt it should be equal pleasure between them. Shasha explained to Doc that her pleasure came from seeing him pleased and satisfied. If only he realized how wet her pussy got from sucking his dick.
Shasha, wet her lips with her tongue to moisten the tip of Docs dick. She moved his dick to the left corner of her warm mouth, to the right corner of her mouth, and gently came down on the head of Doc's dick with her teeth

and pushes all of this dick to the back of her throat and hums with enjoyment. Doc moans and groans, and the further Shasha takes his dick into her mouth, she feels it growing stiffer and longer.

Shasha wants Doc to take her head in his hands and lead the way, hold her head down, and just hold it firmly as his dick got even harder, she knew he was about to cum. Doc, told Shasha, "baby, it is almost there; can you feel it? She could, but all she wanted was to taste him and have him burst all his cum into her mouth. Shasha wanted to see the expression on Doc's face as he gently raises up her head, spit, or swallow.

Shasha, goes to the bathroom, brushes her teeth and uses a little mouth wash, freshen up Ms. Pussy cat and wets a warm towel to get Doc ready for round 3 and a warm towel always feels good afterward. Doc appeared to be enjoying the moment. Memorable. Shasha rested her head on his arm for a few minutes, but she did not want to go to sleep, because Doc won't be able to move. They spooned and relaxed, wrapped up in each other. Doc suddenly roles over on Shasha,

Passionate kisses are exchanged between Shasha and Doc, and she loves the way his kisses make her feel. Her body heats up from head to toe, and her mind goes back to their third night together. Shasha, was thinking damn, he is ready to go again, she reminded Doc that they were both over "20", he gives her a kiss, again and again gently on her lips, on her neck, across the ears, the quaking was upon

Shasha once again, and Doc was headed to the zone. Ms. Pussycat.

Shasha wanted to feel his lips touch the lips of her pussy. it was throbbing, she wanted to feel his lips on her clit, she was anticipating it, she wanted to hear the sounds coming from Doc as he ate her pussy, bending her legs further over her head, taking her hips into his hands, nothing but pussy in his face, as he licks and sucks for a long time, She wanted him in every way and wanted him to have all of her, just spread her legs wide and he could have his way. but, she pulled him back and he paused (sorry babe) and she held his face in her hands and they kissed, their lips and tongue did the tango, his tongue, and her tongue meet and the kiss was deeper (sometimes he takes a few minutes before he lets her pass his tongue) She held his face and pulled him closer (I miss your kiss) he eased inside her hot wet juicy pussy, flood gates were open. The bed was soaked and wet with Shasha's sweat, and she hesitates but explains to Doc, that she did not let him go downtown because she was sweating too much. They rested well for the remainder of the night, but Shasha's body was so hot she could not sleep to close to Doc for the sweating would start once again.

Earlier in the morning, Doc took Shasha on a tour of Charleston to see some of the Historic sites and beautiful scenery. Doc and Shasha went to lunch at one of his favorite spots. His favorite spots but they both had the same favorite meal. After, lunch it was on we were never tired of each other.

The next morning was their last day together for this trip, Shasha had to return to work the following day. She told Doc that checkout was at 11:30, and it was 09:00. So, enough time for one more round.

Doc, it is your turn to tell the story.

Shasha's visit to Doc

Shasha peeked out the window, eagerly anticipating Doc's arrival. She pulled out a table and placed it closer to a more relaxing chair and added another chair for two. A few minutes passed and no knock at the door. She walks over to the window, pulls down the blinds, and he is here. Her heart pounds with intensity as her eyes follow him into the Hotel entrance. Unable to see any further, she goes to the door, waiting for him to knock once, yet she opens the door before he had a chance.

Hello, how are you? Shasha's favorite words to hear, it was music to her ears. She thought that he would want to take a shower, but no, he went to his apartment beforehand. Shasha had the table set up for dinner for two, steak and potatoes with asparagus, and house salad. Sadly, the steak was very well- overdone, to the point that we ordered the Charleston Patties, shrimp with sausage, vegetables, and fried grits.

Small conversations during dinner and he noticed that I had a pedicure, so was he looking at my legs while I was bent over? There was a little wait for the second dinner choice, but all was good. I was still wondering why he was not talking much.

Dinner was over, and now it is time to relax, I was a little tired from the drive, and all I wanted to do was lie in his arms and cuddle for the rest of the night. However, Ms.

Pussycat has a way of letting Shasha know, "no sister girl, we not rolling like that tonight." You did not drive five hours to eat and go to sleep. So, Shasha rolls over to her right side, and he is facing her, and she can feel the heat between their bodies without a touch. She silently wonders why she is so drawn to this man their lips meet, and a long passionate kiss is exchanged. At the moment, her body lightens with ease, and she let out a sigh as she is filled with joy. Doc's kisses warm Ms. Pussycat, every touch of his lips to her moistens Ms. Pussycat, and the faucet was on.

He gently kisses and nibbles on the left nipple; (most sensitive of the two) she quivers, and she shakes, and they kiss longer and deeper. Shasha can't recall how the dress came off or when, but it was gone, he must be a Magician. She rolls over to ride her horse, bumped into a little challenge, but improvised. Her lips found the horse, and she mounted that horse with her wet lips and took all of Doc penis deep down to the back of her throat. As she slowly raised her head up, she went down, tightening those full lips around the rim of his horse. She teased the horsey with her tongue for a long time. Doc was relaxed, laid back, and all he said was hum, hum, hum mm, dam. Of course, those few words just gave Shasha the enthusiasm to work a little harder, and she did, suck his cock as if there was no tomorrow. The more she sucked, the wetter her pussy became, she sucked Doc's dick and enjoyed every second, she could hear the pleasure in his moans, and she wanted him to be satisfied and want all of her in return. Shasha played with her best toy and rubbed her hands back and forth over the head of Doc's dick, and he would lift up of the bed with every forward stroke. Shasha asked, would you like me to stop? His reply was <u>no.</u>

She continued to massage his dick and would add a relief suck so he could relax, sucked his dick just the way she knows he likes it done. There is nothing more passionate than giving deep throat, tongue-twisting, wet lips, and a wonderful hand/rim job.

Doc rolled Shasha, over, baby, I have something for you. She was thinking, give it to me, give it to me, and he did. There were a gentle slide and a thrust, and Shasha felt like she was about to explode, she felt Ms. Pussycat pull Doc's horsey with every movement his body made going deeper, <u>Shasha</u>, was holding on tight for the ride, hungry and thirsty for all of Doc, she was hoping he did not notice that she was on him like she had missed a few meals.

Jimmy

Jimmy just happened to happen, and we met by way of Stephany, a mutual friend. She made a call as a favor, and he came through. We decided on a time and place to go over some material I was working on, and I wanted a second opinion. We met at this Spot in Mid-town that he frequented after work hours. For some reason, I felt compelled to go buy a new outfit and some silver accessories. Picked up this winter white pants suit and a pink blouse just wanted something fresh. I wore some Italian cut shoes a little over 3-inch heels, black with silver trim. My hair was a natural short cut with two strain twists curly faded on the sides and high on the top. I arrived at the location first and got a seat at a table for two. I sent a text message letting him know I was inside the Club.

Jimmy gave me his description, so I recognize him once he entered the Club. He was a published author and wrote erotica. So, that was our mutual interest, and I let him pass by my table. I just wanted to see what he was going to do. He sat at a table for two with high chairs, better for his long legs. I called him on his cell asking, "Where are you?" but I knew. I just wanted to watch him answer...ah, this is like a scene out of a movie, he says, and I smiled, and we introduced our selves. I passed the envelope to him, and he started to review the first 15 pages. I noticed he was wiping his forehead, and he rubs his mustache with two fingers, then he licks his bottom lip. I said Jimmy, by the way, I am watching your reaction to each page. He started to read the next ten pages, but the lighting was poor, so I turned on the light on my cellphone

Jimmy, always had a shit load of questions and I was glad to respond to all he wanted to know. After three months he wanted to know why I left my husband and I responded with he realized my worth too late and the most important reason was I knew my worth. Well, Jimmy confesses his love. I love you, and I am amazed by how much we are similar in behavior, likes, and dislikes. We could be twins. I love what I recognize in you that I know is in me. He wanted to know how anyone could let me go. I explained he fought for me once, so he thinks. My ex-husband started doing the small things I asked him to do, but it was short-lived. I treat people the way I want to be treated, the cardinal rule I show and give Love the way I want to be Loved. Rude and painful awakening, most people don't do the same.

When I left and went to my house, he said nothing. He just expected me to return, and I did not. I gave him more than enough time to come clean on the questions I asked about his sexual preferences. He chose not to, so I tallied all my mental notes up and left never to return. He thinks I will return. Nope, can't get past the man thing. You can't or should not put someone at risk for your selfish desires. Yet he never kissed me, intercourse was out of the question but I was okay with that. I could eat pussy every day, but, but, but.

I was thinking this is different, so I stopped everything. When I have talked, explained, given examples asked questions, and nothing changed, it is time to move on. You want to know if I have any regrets. Jimmy, I have never used that word in any context, I always believe that everything happens for a reason. If you decided you no longer want to have anything to do with me and got back with your ex. I would look at the good that came out of our time together and what did I gain from this experience.

I now have Jimmy in my life, and he was able to communicate his feelings, hold me in his arms, kiss and caress me, tell me what he needs and considerate of mine. He calls all the time just to say good morning and night with I Love You. Wants to know why, just so, sends devotions of love and concern about my safety, etc. Never regrets, I am going to remember you are my Divine gift.

So, committed to you even with medical issues well at some point, we all have or will have medical issues. Besides that, I am a caring and compassionate person. Your wellbeing is important to me. I want you with me for a long time. We have to pay attention to our aches and pains because that's how our body lets us know something isn't right. We are touching all bases, so I point out I notice that he has a specific type of woman he prefers, short and thick women. I know that's what you like, the thinner woman that's good for you, but you are not into slim, as you are into the thick butterball women. He laughs, but I love how you make love to me slapping my pussy with that Big dick you carry on your side, it actually sounds like a slap. When your lips touch my cat, well, you know the rest. So, Jimmy you want to know what to do to please me more. Jimmy, that is easy to answer, don't masturbate because I have to work harder. Well, Shasha, how about you doing something for me…what would that be Jimmy. I want you to display your Nakedness… sorry babe that is going to require some working on. But I will work on it. All the questions in the world did not keep us together, all the I love you and intimate moments wasn't enough. Damn, these lessons are getting powerful. If I was writing this six months ago when I was angry and had some horrifying bad things to say about the dick and how he gave me dick sucking instructions, but I am going to be nice and let stand what I wrote when I was happy. I wanted to kill his dick on paper. So, my happy time is here but silent dialogue was always around. Babe, I hear what you are saying…just to please you I will get a few blow pops and practice the tight sloppy wet drooling seal, (silent dialogue, shit was funny) sound like some instructions I would give. He is concerned about stretching my pussy to far, never heard that one. But. Babe, you are stuck with this pussy from the first time you penetrate. By no means am I fragile or going to break. Now, you want me to open my legs wider, damn you sure are requiring much. The dick is an anaconda, but he is not a wide man, your waist is a 34, why do I need to open my legs wider? You are coming straight forward with room left over.

Shasha, is this real? Jimmy, of course, it's real. Yes, it's real and we are more than lucky with this Love. You can see all of that. Yes, Jimmy I do. The questions continue but he is confused and saying he is a non-believer in Love.

I think, maybe this is your opportunity to renew your belief, it's in front of your eyes, you can see it, feel it, touch it, reach out and take it all, but it's your choice. Proof that no one can spoil Love for you. What's for you is for you. It just happens to be me. I Love You.

If this is real, I am very lucky to have found love again. I am lucky to have someone look at me with desire in their eyes. Jimmy said to Shasha I am a non-believer, so that is why I ask you often why you think you love me. Jimmy you said you appreciate my love for you.

If you appreciate my love for you, then let me Love you, take care of you and your needs. I don't see nor look for weakness in you or your character. Shasha. I felt you were protective of me last night that was new. I am just used to doing it all myself. Jimmy it must be the police officer embedded in you. Shasha, it was scary walking on the streets in downtown Atlanta after midnight to a parking lot and Jimmy I wanted to call an Uber. Yet, you managed to give me the comfort of feeling safe, asking me to watch out for the hole, deep crack, dip off the curb. Come on, Babe, you are my BEST, and I hope I am yours. Things you are worried about or question you ask I never even thought of in any sense. Asking me to drive is not an issue, I was expecting you to, but you didn't, I thought we were going to die. You are an awful driver, and I should have insisted that you pullover. But next time I will, you won't have to ask, it's now an understanding. Between you and me, there is no weakness except how we feel about each other

Shasha, I really appreciate your love for me and I know I have said it before. For some time, I've felt that people who are truly happy are so fortunate. When I said, I wanted you to get to know me better it was for a few reasons. I have been a cop for over 20 years, and I have always been the protector, but sometimes, like when we are out on Friday, I had to rely on you. I felt crushed that I can't be the 100% protector, and it sends me into feelings I would rather not feel. And I want you to know if you feel being a help to me at times when we are out at night, just let me know that it is too much to deal with. I will not take it personally. I will not dislike you for it. My ex was a complete bitch and was insensitive. You are not like her. Thank you. I get scared because my mother just asked me ten minutes ago how my eyesight was. I told her it is maintaining but will never get better. What would happen if it got worse? Like I said Friday, I use to work at Phillips Arena, and I got around quicker and more confident a mere two years ago. What will my sight be like two years from now? I will ask my doctor that tomorrow. I wouldn't want to place a tremendous burden on caring for me like that. Feelings like that make me feel like it is cruel. I don't like it show, but it bothers me. When we were walking outside, and I have to be watchful of dips in the sidewalk or steps, making sure there are 6 steps and not 5. It is obvious, and I don't want people taking advantage of me. When I was driving from the parking deck and for a quick second, I couldn't discern if the wall was 4 feet away in front of my hood or 4 inches was disturbing to me. If someone was behind me, that would have beeped their horn. Then if I ask you to drive at night, it shows my weakness. Safety comes first always.

Driving are bifocals with no line. VA did mine, you are welcome, no analyzing if you want me to know you will tell me, no probing. You are welcome.

Good morning Shasha. I am feeling much better. It seems I can't take all my medication at the same damn time. Ok, Jimmy so I am looking forward to tonight. Shasha, when we get back, hopefully, I can get to bed before 11p.m. I miss seeing you. I am sure as you've figured, some things have been on my mind since that texted message.

Glad you are feeling better, Jimmy. I am as well. Yes, it's been a while, and I do miss you. So how has school been? Great, staying on the President's list. When is your election again? Well, the election is on March 25 by 5 pm. My youngest daughter has a show on March 1, and she is selling tickets. What kind of show is it? It's a Rap concert. She said the purchaser doesn't have to attend the show, but support is definitely appreciated. She doesn't know it yet, but I am going to support her by buying four tix. They are $15.00 apiece. Ok, I will support her as well by getting a few tickets. So sweet of you. Well, I appreciate, over the past week, you haven't been analyzing me. The absence of it sort of makes me feel you don't care, so I know what I appreciate, and what irritates me is one and the same. Anyway, I do appreciate you very much. I do not take that for granted. I don't take your attraction to me for granted. Maybe years ago, I thought I was the shit, but as I get older,

I realize I have been very fortunate to have you feel the way you do about me; unconditionally, so thank you.

Good Night Jimmy... hopes you enjoyed your day off. Did you know that you should follow your heart and not your mind nor someone else's? It's good when we learn and grow and make decisions in accordance with the growth. This means we take into consideration what someone else advised but make our own individual decisions. I hope all is good with you.

I love what you do for me so. You take such good care of me and are so attentive. Okay, so here's the "Happy" issue. I haven't thought about my happiness because of what's going on in my life most particularly, this household. I get scared of telling you what goes through my mind because I don't want you thinking I am not over my ex. As I've said when we first met, I am going through that process and doing much better than I have. At times, I feel like she ruined love for me because I gave so much. And it scares me that she didn't fight for our marriage like I have seen others do. I am apprehensive and wonder if another woman would fight or take flight. I also would like to hear her say, "I wasn't really the one or I really love Todd." Now, I know I won't actually hear her say these words, and I can move on from that. You can help me. You, Shasha, are remarkable. I don't want to lose you, and I had no choice in the time of our lives that we met. Maybe if we would have met around the spring when Saundra would be gone would have helped more and another 3 months under my belt of pushing my ex away would have been our better time, and it would have been sparked galore. Sometimes I get in that rut when I feel like nothing's going my way.

Sometimes, when I have a new girlfriend, I feel a slight difference in my body. This may be a coincidence, but there is a difference. The other night in Conyers and the Hilton was the first time I was really able to "get" at you. When my body enters a new host, it sometimes reacts. Or do you still think I need to take that "shit" pill on Monday night? Yes, please take the shit pill, you will feel light on your feet. Another question, how often is your "often" average? 2X a week? 3x a week? No, you mean a day right. I can hit my vibrator 20 times in about an hour, hollowing and screaming each and every time. But, if that is your cut off, we can work around it. Thank you, Babe, I will give all I have with no short cuts. Shasha, are you always this understandable? Silent dialogue...what the fuck, is this?

Yes, I am always this way unless I am not feeling well, or going through something but I will let you know. You are welcome, and I know if I am not attentive let me know, sometimes I get lost in myself. But, one other thing I want you to know... I love sleeping next to you, and how you cuddle up in your back until you start sweating. I hope all is good between us, this experience is so new to me. Out of my five ex-wives combined, nothing comes close to how you treat me. Do you see any areas where I would need to improve? No need to improve Babe and I have no complaints. Shasha, I wanted you and wanted you with me as much as you would allow. Oh, honey you are my best! Of course, I am. You know I am going to bring your

nourishment; this massive dick is ready to quench your thirst. I know you thirsty, your lips look a little dry, come on over here you need to be replenished. Thank you for paying attention to my unconditional Love for you.
Shasha you take such good care of me. I sometimes wonder, are you always like this? I haven't had a chance to show you generosity. You keep doing new stuff. You care for me medically, feed me, attend to me and pleasure me. When I was sick and in the Hospital, you come back when you had a break to pleasure me. Who does that? You. LOL. I thank you for so much attention. I Love sleeping with you. You are comfortable to lay next to. You don't complain that you got to get some sleep... like last night when I kept you up late. You stayed up late to greet me and pleasure me. You brought me breakfast and lunch, which will be my dinner. Thank you.

Shasha, I have been thinking a lot about you. I was nervous that first time. At my age, sometimes, I may have difficulty in staying hard. Hopefully, when we get more comfortable, I will get over that. We did not get into different positions. I came quick. Your rim Shasha got me to the edge multiple times. It is easy to get hooked on those. I need to hear your fuck voice again. You have a low pitch voice, but I am interested in hearing it again.

Babe, don't rationalize I have no complaints. I can get you over the edge and empty if you save it for me. It can be intense, especially if I continue while you are cumin. So, what were you thinking about when you were thinking about me a lot? How is your back? Will you be able to get a heating pad? I could get you one, and you meet me at the gas station. I Love You.

Loving you back, since making love, you've been in my mind. Your kisses and rim Shasha are phenomenal. I have never felt anything so intense so many times in my life. The mixture of pleasure and pain was superb. I could get hooked on that. I try not to think of it too much because it is addictive. So, you say trial and error got you to the expert level you're at now, huh? Trial and error. Interesting to ponder what was your first rim Shasha like. It was amazing because I think I'd prefer the rim Shasha over puss, but the jury is still out on that. I don't want to get too greedy with those because I can see myself waking you up just for a rim Shasha and nothing else. I must be decades since the last time my body shuddered like that.

It was hard to focus at work you stayed in my mind; I couldn't shake the thoughts running through my head from last night. So, today wasn't the most productive day, but I got some cases closed. Most of the cases I touched needed additional information, so I had to send a Check List letter out to the Veteran. I did get your texts, but the last text said you have something for me. Is it more of last night? Later on, first Jimmy this is where we left off from last night before you got deep in me. I don't think you move to fast, and you just let the wrong people choose you. Getting to know you… well I feel we are coming along, just a few rough patches for you, but we will survive them. You gave me a few examples of recreating scenarios with your ex's. I am okay with that if you are just telling me and not acting out without me knowing to see my response.

You said your ex, isn't an issue for you? However, from the examples you gave last night between you and the two ex's one was not out of line for thinking that you let the other run you or the house... my perception. The ex needs to stay in her place, but she has no more control than you give her in your life. Besides, you can't use circumstances such as possible danger and the child being at home as the reason for you to go to her. Not making a case for your second ex, yes, I would be upset, but I would have handled it differently. We going together. I don't want to make the same mistakes with you as I have in my past relationships, I don't want to lose you.

Jimmy, I don't want to lose you, neither Babe, but how would you feel if Chris called his kids or me because he was sick in the hospital or even at home. He may just want me to sit with him for a little while because I am a nurse. But you and I have plans, and I ask you to wait ... put a hold on our plans. I will be back shortly, and I drove to Jonesboro to his house that we use to live in together and did husband and wifey shit. Usually, if you want to know how the other person may feel about your actions, weight how you would feel if it happened to you, often, we treat people the way we want to be treated, at least I do.
Jimmy, I am excited as well about us, and it feels so scary good. Like something bad is going to happen to happy. But I accept it all, past time for me to be happy. I am sure things will change for the better and remember that ups and

downs come with the territory. Thanks Babe, we are both catches, I am thankful that we both love each other.

Oh Jimmy, I already really, really love you, and there is always room for the heart to grow fonder. Mine is open. Shasha, I just have to ask you this one more time... you went on your lunch break to get married. Yes, I went on my lunch break and got married, but it was a month after I got engaged. So, was it more of an open marriage? Yes, but only that I came and went as I pleased. I am sure he didn't appreciate it. We sort of did our own thing. I would stay a few weeks and go home for a few days. He would get on my last nerves, that unspoken language of wanting to say something but don't. Enough about that... you asked if I think you are nasty in bed.

I won't think you are nasty, if you don't want me to but Babe, you are freaky nasty. I get Horney just thinking about what you do to me with that special finger. That's why I got my vibrators on stand- by, to take the edge off when I can't get to you. I stopped using them for a while, you are aware I only like the bullet, no longer or bigger than my thumb. Perfect for buzzing my clit. Yes, Shasha but we can lay it to rest, right and you just come and get it.

Have you told your family about us? They are privilege to know I am seeing you, your address, cell number and car tag number, safety first. Really, that is not funny, but I got it. This is my time for me to do the best for myself and fulfill my soul desires they have always been with me. You are what's best for me, just as you are, just be yourself. I love every aspect of you, just don't take anything away. Jimmy, take a few deep breaths and breathe; it is all going to be great. God, you & me, sex and family. I Love you, and only you, no questions asked. I know my worth and yours, and we are worthy of each other. I think, I might be experiencing cold feet…silent dialogue…got damn it.

Hi Shasha. just retouching again on the "cool" feet. Nervous about the unknown. You want to know why? Well, because 2017 and 2018 were not good years for me regarding relationships. In hindsight, I moved too fast, and I ended up regretting it people ended up not liking me so much. I definitely want you to get to know me, and I am aware that as time goes on, this will take place. I want to recreate past scenarios to let you see what it is to deal with Barbara and me (silent dialogue, hell no, to the no, no, no). Because the other ex-wives aren't an issue. I want to recreate scenarios that upset Ana and also see if I handle them better, or was it all in her mind. You are so remarkable, and I don't want to lose you, but more importantly, I don't want you regretting anything. I am excited about you and I, and then I get a little bit nervous about how will things change. Will things change? I like that we live close to each other, but then again, I hate Lithonia. You are making improvements to your home. You are such a catch, and I always am thankful that you love me, but I want to see if you really love me and if there's more room for you to love me (silent dialogue, holy shit).

I get nervous I am scared you may think I want it too much 2 to 3 times a week. I fully understand the exercise you gave me of the shaded and remaining boxes. I have never dated a woman in the amount of time we've been dating and *haven't* been intimate. What if you are too much for me? What if you aren't? What if I am not what you expected? Not that my manhood is threatened because I have nothing to prove at my age or even if I was 35 for that matter. I don't know. Can you help me? I am trying to be what's best for you. You have so much going on with school and all. I don't want to add to anything. Silent dialogue…I am dating myself, oh my God…just don't say a word.

You say that you love me. Why? I apologize if my actions sometimes don't match my words. In addition to the obvious, I sometimes get cool feet. I know you're the best thing that's happened to me and you take care of me. The funny thing when we were at the suite, you said when I got hot under the covers, I threw the covers off of me, exposing my top half. It's an unconscious habit. You got to see some of me, but you were covered up like a nun in the other bed. I saw no shoulders, no elbows, no knees, no thigh, no stomach, no hips, nothing. So that's what gives me cool feet because you make me feel like I am the one who's rushing you, and you are uncomfortable with it. No, Babe you are over thinking, but it is okay to go through it this way if it helps you to get past your fears.

Good morning Shasha, I *enjoyed* seeing you. Last night was so different. Your new look is very nice! The cut, the color, the heels; all FANTASTIC. Your lips? The fullest. The softest. And I wanted to thank you again for creating a book club. I appreciate you on so many levels. I also think it was so sweet and protective of you when you mentioned a woman you did not tell about my book because you felt she would "hunt" me out? I appreciate that. But uh, what about me. You don't have faith in me to recognize the obvious "if" she were to locate me. But it's your call. I trust your judgment. I also enjoyed our talk last night, referencing the History Channel and man's purpose on earth. DNA structure and the relation to life in this galaxy before us. It is mind-blowing to assume we are the only living creatures in existence. Were there others before us? Are we being watched? Are our leaps in technology predestined? If mankind starts going off track from the divine footprint, what takes place to get mankind back on track? Imagine if we today are actually prehistoric? Mind-blowing to see ancient remains throughout the world. What did they witness? Is space travel from other galaxies common? Was Earth visited years ago?

Babe, of course, I have faith in you and that you are capable of identifying the undesirables. If I see a rattlesnake coming, I am not going to wait until it strikes before I kill it…I am making the first move.

One other thing Shasha, were you at the Basketball game last night, it looks like I saw a post of you at the game. And I am a little mad at you. I saw on social media that you were at the Hawks game. Now, I remember you told me about tix some time ago, but I forgot. Then you asked me to come out for a few but didn't say anything about the Heat and ATL game. If you said something Saturday, I would have mentally prepared myself for it (silent dialogue, just let me beat my own ass, right here).

Don't be upset, sorry about that... I did mention it, rather asked you and I did look for a ticket, but there was none in close proximity to my seat. I really did not want to go to the game alone, but I did not want to waste the free ticket. It was Atlanta and the Heat, and it was boring. I will make up for it.

Ok, well, I need to ask you about Ana and Pam, just getting the elephant out of the room. You said they are different? Wat did you mean? And you might stop communicating with Ana at some point. What are you hoping for from Ana? I need to know if this is something, I need to release myself from.

Shasha, okay to hopefully address your last concerns. About Pam wife # 5, quick and easy, "Hell Fucking No". There is no steamy chapter going down where she's in the kitchen, and I reach for a cup. When I think about being near her, it makes me mad. The other day after she pulled that false alarm shit, she asked for a ride to a store because it was inaccessible by bus. I told her ass before to get Zelle on her phone and download Uber. But I took her quickly and couldn't wait for her to get out of my car. I don't like being in close proximity to her! If there she was the only woman on the planet, I still wouldn't fuck with her. She lies, and I can't stand that shit. I don't trust her, and wife #3 Barbara told me that she is out for blood. Talking shit about her being a Christian, and I am the one who is making her the bitch she used to be. How in the world can I make you revert back to a bitch and forget all your bible verses? So, NO is the answer to that shit.

Barbara is one that we can't live under the same roof and Pam is another one, times ten. Talking shit about me in front of my daughter was the last straw. Last Saturday, she called me at work, staying where was a Marshal at the front door. Her details about their conversation sounded fishy. She asked me if I was serving her with papers. I said no. She said she was nervous. I said I don't know who it was. There have been times she will lie about the simplest things, and that lurks my nerve. I showed her how to set the alarm, and she's been doing it correctly for a year, then all of a sudden, she trips the alarm.

My mother sent me a Xmas package with a few items in it, and I haven't received the package yet. I think Pam may have intercepted it. I have order items online that are missing including your gift. I inform her that the status of my items says delivered, but I don't have them. She'll reply she hasn't seen them. Today while at work, she texted me saying a package arrived for me. It was a book I ordered. I call Amazon, told them I never received it and they sent me a duplicate on this past Friday. Is this book the first book I ordered or the 2nd one? And on a Sunday? Oh, so the other day when she was at work, I got home, and there was a package for her. I thought it was my gift for you, but it wasn't. I took and hid her package until my package shows up. She asked me if I see her package because the status shows her that it was delivered. I played dumb just like she did, so no, there is no doubling back and trying to make it work with her.

She is a liar and underachiever. Funny thing is when I first met her. I thought she was bougie. From the bathroom near the dining room, I can overhear her on her phone talking about me. I pay every single bill in this house, and she pays nothing. Now, I know what you may be thinking. I recently said to myself I will let it ride, and she can save her money to help her move. But I pay every bill, and she has the nerve to talk shit about me? She's greedy. For food shopping, we do go to the market because she can't carry many bags on the bus, so I take her. She will ask for the budget, and she always goes over the budge. The food shopping before Xmas I told her the budget was $200. The bill came out to $307.00 The following week she said she had to pick up more items for Xmas dinner, which I was not home to eat, nor wanted any of it anyhow and that was another $60 and I thought since she said "she" had to go the market, she was going to pay for it. I was mad again as fuck. Almost $400 in food purchases. She drank two bottles of Tropicana OJ in two weeks like I got an orange tree in my backyard.

But I promised myself there would be no more food shopping. She can pick up things as needed, and I will pick up things as needed, but no more driving together to Walmart. She has a cold and texted me saying she ate one of my soups and will repurchase a soup. I flipped. Are you going to buy me a soup? What about the OJ you drank? She said to buy another one, and she promised not to drink it.

Of course, I have yet to bring any OJ in this house (silent dialogue, he is serious, not going to interrupt...but this shit is funny).

Shasha you are a remarkable woman. The incident that took place at my house the other day makes me feel less than remarkable. I don't do drama. Yet the drama was at my front door. I am still pissed over that. I feel my eyes wide open in mild shock regarding you saying this woman isn't playing. The other side of me says I got to get this shit completed before I present myself to you. The reason I am still pissed is because she set the alarm off that led to my daughter being called and me missing 8 calls from her that led to getting her mother and coming over to this house that led to Pam opening her mouth and saying things that should not have been said in front of my daughter that led to Barbara and Pam exchanging phone numbers. Barbara says it's, so when Pam calls her, she can report back to me anything crazy Pam says. So, then Barbara reports back to me and tells me things Crazy Pam talks about. In the past day or two, Barbara has said Pam knows too much about me. I told Barbara, Pam and I were married for 15 months, of course, she's going to know something about me but Barbara says Pam is telling her how much debt I owe and what I have in my TSP. But Barbara will tell Pam she knows what my debts because it's no secret. So, know I am dealing with a person who wants to open her mouth when she shouldn't. This leads me to me staying out of the house. I know I am not married to either one of them, but if I stay out, she will call Barbara to cry (report) on her shoulder, and then Barbara may repeat something in front of my daughter, where my daughter feels all men lie. I've told you the relationship my daughter and I have; I don't want her feeling a certain kind of way about my men and me as a man and her father. So now I look at Pam as the ultimate snake, and I wish her to be gone out of my house immediately. But I realize I am on the cusp of your love. I see you like taking care of your man. You are thoughtful. Very thoughtful. I want to offer you the same back, especially a drama free friendship/life (silent dialogue, toxic shit...I am going to follow it a while longer).

Jimmy, guess I can still say that you are a remarkable man "shit happens" we all experience drama at some level and points in our life. Be thankful that was your first with a few wows so look at it as if it was a lesson and what did you learn and you will feel better about the entire situation. It wasn't your drama...it was the drama of others. Don't be pissed rise above it elevate your vibration, play some more music reminisce about something that made or makes you happy. The comment "this woman isn't playing" you indicated I said. I don't recall saying it, or for what reason, I would have said it. But if I wrote it, I will look back on it to see why.

So, you have to get your situation together before you present yourself to be confusing because I felt you had already completed that presentation. I understand how you feel about the alarm and 8 missed phone calls, but honey, we all play a part in the toxic events that occur in our lives. Some are due to the toxic people that we continue to allow to play big roles in our life. Don't be upset when I say this, but how do you think it would have played out if you had answered the phone or checked it when I brought it to your attention. Sure, you did not want to hear that, but there is a lot of room for but's and what ifs here.

Another point could be that everything happens for a reason; rather, it's a lesson or exposure of a snake or just to open your eyes to something you needed to see. Maybe, you should have that talk with your daughter while she is in her feelings, woman perception. You took the long roads and went around the corner to get to "staying out of the house." Well, I must say you do spend nights out of the house when you travel out of town, or when you are going to a function and may stay late. But, correct me if I am wrong, no drama or emergency events that cause any type of upset ever happened. Another "but" when you just happen to spend the night with me, not all day into the early morning just the hours you slept through-out the night in the bed next to mine all hell breaks loose. You took the words out of my mouth, and you are not married to them, so why do you let them have that much of a hold on you? Just asking. Shasha, I don't know how to respond to the last sentence, but I will make an attempt. Jimmy before you respond, listen and read out loud the email that you just sent me. I am feeling some kind of way about the parts that pertain directly to you and me.

Please, don't try me or provoke a negative response from me. Please Babe, don't be like that. Don't put any. Yours is greater than mine tag it on nothing, I give if I have it, and I don't put a thought to a purchase or think it's too early to buy a gift of taste. Are you promising for the next five minutes to just listen? No, you are not. I know your worth and you should recognize it as well. So, accept the gifts and don't bring my vibes down. It felt good these past few days can't we just focus on loving each other. (silent dialogue, my God, he is broken).

In the future, I am confident that you will buy me something that's going to surpass what I got you for Xmas. The phone ringing by no means was I tracking your incoming phone? It was an innocent observation, as in, it may have been important because it kept ringing. I know when my phone continues to ring, it's important. Be mindful of your tone with me, respectfully. When it comes to your family, you know what you should do, and that is your decision.

But you should consider cutting some strings with a few wives, and your life would be a little easier. All the emails we have shared and all the expectations you have shared, I expect the same in return from you. God first, you the man, and please, speak/talk to me like I am the person you are in Love with, not angry 😠 with. Before you send it, read over it, question how would this be received?
Let's not self-sabotage if you don't want this, it's ok. Just say the word because I prefer to stay on my high.

Shasha, I am sorry, I woke up this morning immediately, knowing I was not in that comfortable bed of room 440. Again, thanks go much. I want to tell you that the more I think of the value of the gifts, I feel that I can't accept it. I

187 of MEN IN MY BED

got you something I think you would really like, but the value is not as much as your gift, and I am feeling uncomfortable when I compared your earrings to mine, even though it dawned on me the value. Even the value of the cologne I can imagine was steep. If I paid $100 for Tom Ford and was half the size of Gucci, then I realize you spent some coins on me. So, I am feeling a bit uncomfortable. (silent dialogue, karma, karma, karma…because I would have been gone by now…done).
So, unless there was a remarkable sale at Macy's, I would like to talk to you about the gift. I do appreciate you so very much for digging deep in your purse for a gift of that magnitude so early.

(silent dialogue, dig deep…hum). This Tuesday, I am going to U-Haul and buy some boxes and let her see that I am slowly packing. I got to ask her once I give her money, when does she think she'll be leaving for good. Barbara and I have kids, so she and I will always have to talk. Pam and I don't have kids, and once she's gone, there will be no reason to talk. Ana and I don't have kids, but it's different than Pam, but one day it two will be at a place when we don't talk. Well, I think that was therapeutic for both of us. That was so much emotion. Let's change this to dick and pussy, get this tightness out of my neck.

Yes, Babe we defiantly can change this shit up…I noticed that you like grabbing my ass when I am deep inside your pussy, when I am standing up and you are sucking my dick. I love how you suck my dick as long as it is any kind of way other than slow. I would like for you to already be naked when you arrive next time. Your specifications are reasonable and achievable to the fullest.

I have a few stipulations for you to follow, I like my clit sucked and make that smacking noise, like it is the coochie you have ever ran your lips across. Question? Have never identified what type of Lover you are based on my skills and other lovers' critique. Hell no! (silent dialogue…got to be patient!)

This was scary, the picture you painted of your ex-wives, but funny at the end. No apology needed because you are already aware that I feel you are avoiding me, and you are sending mix messages, which you cleared up a little bit today.

I have a few more comments:
1. All I am giving is unconditional love, respect, and understanding
2. Your wives and children don't know of me, no drama for me
3. So, where is the drama in this for me? It's indirectly not directly and all for you
4. Now, if we all were introduced to each other there would be a few shifts
5. Hiccups and growing pains would cover all aspects of us
6. It sounds like you are saying bye and thank you
7. The highest vibration in the Universe is Love, who doesn't want that experience
8. If you are saying bye and thank you.

I am not sure how or if you wanted me to answer the above questions.

1) All I am giving you is unconditional; are these your words or mine?

2) Correct. They don't know about you, so no drama for you.

3) No drama for you. If any, it would be indirectly.

4) Introduced to each other? Huh

5) Ture comment

6) No, I am not saying goodbye and thank you.

7) Vibrations. I understand

8) Same as #7

Number 1 is from me; number 3 you are correct; it would be indirectly. Yes, introduce all your ex-wives to the new woman. Since I am on the topic of ex's, do you have a need to keep them so near and dear? You leave room for things to happen that wouldn't have ordinarily come about. For example, anyone of them is in the kitchen washing dishes, and you reach around to get a cup, and she turns around, and you all just happen to kiss, and it all goes down on the kitchen floor. They were your wives, and sometimes husbands and wives dabble as exes. No, I am not doing that number 7 ok? You are not saying goodbye and thank you, appreciate that. Now, the divorce from Pam, any regrets? Would you reconsider since she is still there, and you are getting over Ana? Hell No! Yes, I do recall everything you said regarding both of them. But are you reading all of my emails to you because I explain why?

I think I understand your case of CSI, but it would be nice if you could explain it again, I may have missed something. Failed relationships help us to be the person we show up as today, lessons. Look at amazingly wonderful you! The hotel room I was covered because of what you said take it slow. I didn't want it to appear that I did not hear you or understood your intent. I was naked under the covers, and I turned around, and your covers were at your waist or lower, I wanted to, but your words stayed on my mind, I suffered in silence and watched you sleep for a while.

You have nice a physic, I like your pecs, and I want to feel and taste you. I regret missing the moments because it seems that they are at the forefront now, which may cause more of a hindrance. Well, the "if's" if it was awkward you would pull away, really that's extreme. Why did you get back to your bed? I had already asked at the movies. I usually ask the man I am interested in what he likes and how he likes to make Love. I don't like missing a beat. If it is hot and steamy with soaking wet sheets and you fucking me so hard, I have to bury my face in a pillow to keep the neighbors from hearing my passionate screams. Having your face between my legs and you come up and we kiss long and deep, until I can taste my own juices. Getting you to the edge and watching you cum all over my breast, like you like to. I just want that good old fashion fuck. The weakness in the knees, the hot soaking tub bath and the walk of pain for the next week. Something to keep you on my mind and me on yours, I feel we could have that (Shit is about to get real).

Shasha, again I apologize for not having the endurance to come back out once I am in. I seldom come back out once I am in. But I was tempted. To answer a previous question, how would Xmas eve be different if I did get my daughter's call? Easy. She would have known I was not in danger and would not have come to my house. But seeing who the snake was is an eye-opener. I guess I get weary of the drama. (silent dialogue...damn right).

 The drama that could have been avoided if she and I didn't divorce, but then I wouldn't have met you. I get nervous because all I have seen was failed relationships after Ana and I divorce. I don't want you hating me. I seem to get inconsistent when I over-think us (silent dialogue, sure enough).

With Pam, I want her out as soon as yesterday. Ana used to complain that Barbara use to "run" me. That's where it ends. Then we have you, which says to cut the ties loose from Ana completely
(No, I said all of them).

I also get nervous because I don't want to seem selfish, although it may be just that. When we were at the hotel, we chilled and had a great time, slept in the same room as if cousins. You were respectful and covered. You did mention at the movies that I could sleep in your bed, but when we got back to the room, you didn't gently insist on it when I got back in my bed (silent dialogue... oh, my fucking God) and like I said, when I held you and kissed you, I felt you pulled away because of shyness or maybe properness, and I didn't overpower you, so I left it alone (silent dialogue, don't recall that on, but ok).

Once you did that, I felt odd. You asked if I was coming back, stating the third time would be basically different. I didn't want to take a chance that night. The other part of sacredness comes into play like this. What if we did make love, and you are very different from what I am used to? I like erotic sex and what if you're more reserved (silent dialogue, this has to be karmic). What if you suck my dick, all soft and slow, and I need fast and deliberate and sloppy techniques? Well, then...guess you would have to stay around to find out.

One half says, you have an imaginative mind, and the other half says, you may be able to write erotica, but unable to act it out. I am scared if you give yourself to me, and I feel like I was making love to the preacher's wife, I will feel awkward and pull away. (silent dialogue, all I can do is shake my mother fucking head). What if I am nervous and I can't perform? (silent dialogue, ah the golden question). I think one half says you are so reserved and mild, but in bed, you may blow my mind. Do I take that chance? You may be the best lover I have ever had in my life. You may be vocal and submissive, and you may need a quiet church mouse.

And when you tell me things like 3rd times a charm or other cute quotes, it makes me all the more nervous. You may be a cougar in bed, or you may be a kitten. All I know is I go through my mood swings of horny as fuck, then mild horniness. I want you to grab my ass as I am deep in you. Kiss me with eyes open as we fuck. Suck my dick as you look at me. Hold my head in place as I eat your pussy. Look over your shoulder as I fuck you from behind. I may feel disappointed if you place gentle kisses on my stomach, taking forever to place my dick in your mouth. I am not the 50 Shades of Grey type of lover. ((silent dialogue, old shit now, sounding like my kind a man...but I am not saying shit). I am the Chasing Waterfalls type of lover. My book will tell you exactly what I am used to and what I like. I am nervous that you may look at me different like I am too nasty. When we were at the Hotel, it was clothing on until we showed, then there was sleep attire. Next time you're there, and I get there after you, I would appreciate you already naked and comfortable. You take fantastic care of me, standing vertical. In my novelist mind, I would hear you say, "Do you want to suck on my pussy now or after you eat your dinner?" ((silent dialogue...I do, I do).

I would like to ask you a question Shasha, but I get very nervous about it. Go ahead and ask. So, would you ask for some loving? Yes, I would, but since you are so sweet and fine, you don't have to ask just make the move.

How about asking for some before they marry. Jimmy, I think it should at least be a three times quota. Of course, sex is good before marriage, need a test drive. Well unfortunately, I think younger couples may look at ... oh this is all I can have for the next 30/40 years. Sex is good at all ages, but again, I think older couples look at other aspects of marriage first. For example, if the husband became ill, can the wifey hold down the responsibilities of the household and take care of the husband? Depends on the type of wife you marry.

I had this question answered. When a woman dates, she knows pretty much immediately if she is going to sleep with the guy. As a woman, Jimmy I can say that thought holds some water. A guy only hopes he will have an opportunity and won't have a clue until the clue is given. If a woman says she wants to sleep with a man before they marry because she wants to know if he's well, is that fair? Well, you mean if his dick works, is it too small, that kind of well is fair.

On day I saw a man put both hands as fist, and one of his foot in a huge pussy. She was hollowing and screaming, he took out his dick and it looked like it belonged to an eight-year-old. He rubbed it right at the tip of the giant pussy orifice that now I am sure he could have rested his in. I was stunned. Because, she was brave to even let him see it. Don't need any traumatizing experiencing on the wedding night. So, yes, a man can and should ask for "some" to see if it's good before they marry. I have heard more women than men say they want to know if it's good before marriage.

Yep, and I have heard women say they would cheat if they're not satisfied! It is true, at least for me but more than likely I would leave. In today's world, it's fair, I think because some men and women would let this be one of the determining factors as to rather, they actually marry the person or if they will cheat on the spouse.

Now, an update from my camp. You had said someone was blowing up my phone. The truth was multiple people were calling me. After we got back from the movies and you even called my phone, my alarm company called me. It seems that Pam carelessly set the alarm at 1:00 a.m. in the morning. The alarm company called me. I missed the call, then they called my daughter, my daughter called me and got no response, and she got worried, then her and her mother went to my house and confronted Pam, not knowing if I was okay or not. When I left the Hotel and put in my nephew's address, I saw the missed calls and multiple texts. I explained to my daughter and her mother and apologized for worrying them. They were at my door at 2 a.m. along with the police. Needless to say, when I got home, there were a few words exchanged about her carelessness and having the police respond for the 3rd time within 4 months and worrying my daughter to the point she got her mother out of bed. I asked Pam why did she leave the house at that hour if she is scared to walk from the bus stop after work at 1 p.m. She said she needed dishwashing liquid to wash the dishes. At 1 a.m. in the morning? I was furious. So, my daughter and her mother got out of their beds, and the police dispatched because she needed dishwashing liquid. I told Pam when I apply for my TSP load and give her money, how soon could she be gone. Pam tells me, my ex-wife, Barbara, was sympathetic to her situation. I had to remind Pam that she would never sympathize with the woman who slept with her husband. I am also pissed because I didn't really care for exposing the BS in my household that particular day.

Things are typically quiet, then all of a sudden, my daughter has to respond to my house on what she thought was some domestic violence. The reason I am pissed because just the day before, I asked her Barbara why Karen isn't dating, and she said, "She just isn't. No particular reason, and I know she really doesn't trust men." So, I said I would have a talk with her on Christmas day. I was not trying to push her to have a boyfriend, but just ask her thoughts on why she doesn't trust men, then this shit happens at my house involving me. So obviously I can't have that talk with my daughter any time soon. That was the first time Karen, her mother, and Pam met face to face. Karen didn't care much for Ana; she doesn't like Pam, for obvious reasons. And as I reviewed my call log when we were taking a nap, and you said no bill collectors call that late, that call at that hour was Pam. Now I don't like it when my phone is clocked by others, so please don't do that. BTW, if a bill collector calls from the West coast, there is that 3-hour time zone difference.

But if it makes you uncomfortable if and when my phone rings, I can simply plan early outings with you. Ana calls as I have said with her there is nothing to report about her phone calls. Pam may call, but only if something needs my immediate attention. Her calling Tuesday was a fluke, and Barbara may call also, but it isn't every day.

I have had enough of this toxicity for today. So, Babe, let me tell you what I had my hopes up high for on New Year's Eve. I wanted to make up for Christmas. So, I got the King Suite, got your Champagne, and it was chilling. Got me some Baileys and shrimp cocktail, and some nuts, and baby oil, Vaseline, and water. Black lace short nightie nakedness underneath just hoping you would show. But I did not want you to feel I was rushing you to make love to me, and you were not ready. So, I slept then woke up and had some nutrients. So, is it okay if I just climb on top? I Love You... (silent dialogue, stepping out...player). Before we get started on me, let's explore these questions:

We spend a lot of time on my issues, Shasha lets revisit yours. Jimmy, I don't care to revisit my past, that's why it's the past. I need a better understanding of how they let you go. Okay, if you must.

So, Shasha, you say he got closure, but you didn't. Are you okay with that? Has he tried reaching out to you since then? If he hasn't, but he reaches out to you next year, what would you do? Although I know it's difficult to answer that, try to answer it. How invested were you? Did you guys talk about marriage? Throwing yourself into your work is one way to get your mind occupied. I am sure with your background you can offer self-therapy. How does that work? Has Andrea been offering you any good advice? The lesson you speak about did resonant with me: realizing self-worth. If it helps you to talk about it with me, I can listen. So, you say if someone showed interest, you would be willing. I read this book called the 5 love languages. I learned a lot from that book on how to talk and listen.

Practice makes perfect though. Genuineness in love is definitely important. I know I also learned a lot about what I want and what I will tolerate and not tolerate in a relationship.

But you asked in a text which ex-wife am I waiting for to run back into my arms. The reason I say open to a friendship is because I didn't want to put myself out there. We met because of our love for writing. I don't want to be anyone's follow-up. I want my next relationship to be on solid ground and not just sex in the beginning because beyond sex, I want that Ashford and Simpson type of love. Shit, this is my last quarter. But I realize that after sending you pix last night, it may have taken us from building a friendship to the sex zone. Which I wouldn't mind, but I also want something more solid along with that. I want to build. I want you to know more about me. Maybe I am not all that you thought. I still work on my self-esteem issues, as you can tell. But I want to be "the one" to someone. That person that "does" it for them. May I share a story with you? Okay, with an ex of mine, one night, she was in bed waiting on me to finish showering. She was in bed messing with her phone. When I came out of the bathroom, she sat up quickly and placed her phone on the nightstand. That look in her eyes was like; finally, he's finished showering. Now come here, lover. I want that effect on my future wife all the time. What my desires are and what I want to do as a couple would be discussed if I spark someone's interest. I am open to more than a friendship too if you like what you see. I don't know if you're just being sweet, polite.

Jimmy, I think you are handsome, nice shiny bald head and awesome smile and the walk (Yes, I genuinely do notice). I am not business-like unless it's with the higher-ups, and it's necessary. Sometimes, I am laid back with them. My title in the Union, well, some see it as power and that it is, but I don't let it go to my head. One or two crazy bone stories on Channel 2 News, I will tell you one day when you want to be entertained.

So, you are not over Ana, and you are not waiting on her to return. What if she decides to return New Year's Day because she realizes you are her one, how forgiving will you be then?

Well, my situation with Doc isn't even a situation. Just something stuck in my heart that only time will work out. Like a splinter deep in my foot, you can pick part of it out but it may break off and go deeper but it's not safe to pick any further. Let it rest, but as you wash your feet and it heals from the inside, eventually it will come on out.
I said all of that in the last passage to show it's been happening since last year things with Doc. I did not just start this process with him.

I am okay with that because it was the third time something of that sort had occurred. I made a visit to him in April 2018 for three days. The first day was good and the second. However, on the third morning around 06:00, he was getting ready for work but stated that he was tired. I suggested that he call in. His reply was, "I can't call out, I have used all my time with my son and his basketball." So,

MEN IN MY BED

he decided to stay an hour or two later, but someone kept calling every 30 minutes. He said it was a co-worker, and then he wanted to know what time I was leaving. I wasn't sure, so I said probably late.

He left around 07:30, and I called for a late check out at 13:00. There was a little hand on stuff before he departed. It's okay when someone tells me something my man is doing behind my back because I am not going to say anything to him about it. I will just make a mental note. So, I set the alarm for 1200 noon and went back to sleep. When the alarm went off, I got up and took a showered, regular hygiene regimen. Got dressed, was wearing a short Linen gray dress with spaghetti straps and black sandals with 2.5-inch heels. Short curly hair cut/blonde, legs long, and all oil up.

We were at the Hilton Garden Inn North Charleston, and a few restaurants were on the strip. His *job* was 3 miles from the Hotel, so nice me, I texted, checked out, and noticed it is lunchtime. I made a decision to bring him lunch. I waited for a reply, and there was none. So, I rationalize for him, oh he must be in an area with bad phone reception because it has happened. I texted again, "I got you a tropical chicken salad with shrimps and an ice tea. Be there in 10 mins." Still no response. I picked up the food and drove to his job. Texted again, "I am outside," no response, then a man comes out of the building. I asked, "do you know Doc?" and he said, "yes." "Can you tell me if he is at work today?" and his reply was, "yes, I can answer that?

No, Doc is not at work today. He went to his son's game." I said, "Okay, thank you," and I left.

So, I have always disregarded all the times in the last two years that his brother shared his doings with others. But when I catch you in a lie, it is definitely different. This was not the first lie or mishap. I usually stayed between 3 to 8 days with him. Another mishap occurred in 2017; a few days had gone by, and I promised to cook for him each day. I asked what he wanted, and it something like baby lima beans, fried chicken, so I made that with rice, cornbread, and mac/cheese with leftovers. After he got off from work and came in, it was damn sure it smells good in here. The food was still warm enough. He did not need to heat up anything. The next day was seared pan steaks with grill corn on the cob and baked potatoes. Must be something about the third day, he gets up, fixed him a cup of coffee, and asked if I would like one and which flavor. So, I said hazelnut, and I would add my own sugar and cream. He walked over to the dishwasher and pulled out a huge mug. I noticed red lipstick on the outside of the cup and the inside, one perfect lip print. I watched him fix the coffee and still did not notice the print. He sits back reading the newspaper and starts the word puzzle. So, he sees that I am not drinking the coffee and ask if it was okay. I said, well, I am bothered by the lipstick print on the cup because I have no idea where those lips probably could have been.

Doc was hesitant for a brief moment and came with, "I don't know what you are talking about." Therefore, I showed him the hot red lipstick print on the cup. Oh, a friend came by for coffee as they were passing through town. My question to him was what happened to I-Hop or Waffle's house and who wears hot red lipstick at 07:30 in the morning, and you get off at 07:00. I got up and went into the bathroom, got dress, and was about to leave, and he said, "where are you going?" I did not say a word, just sat on the side of the bed looking cute. He went back into the kitchen. I pulled out my Real-estate book and started d to read a chapter. He came back and sat next to me on the bed: his words, "you are married, what am I supposed to do? Just sit here and wait on you? I am a man, and I can't offer you what your husband is offering you. I explained my circumstances to you, don't get me wrong, and it is not just the sex." Things add up, and I give chances after chances to a fault. Long story short, you already know about the last trip. I am okay with it.

Has he reached out to me since then?
Yes, I heard from him since the last visit in Charleston.
If he reaches out to me next year, he may reach out to apologize, if he does, I will accept his apology, and that will be it, the horse is dead, and I don't hold grudges. I always told him do you, be yourself. I look for growth, realization, and correction in behavior. He made some adjustments. Besides, I keep in mind his own suggestions. He stated that my husband was not going to change, that he was just doing what he thought I wanted and would revert back to his old ways. He was correct, so I believe he will also continue to be dishonest and deceitful when actually there was no need to.

I decide if I want to stay or go, and it is on my own accord. I felt I was invested enough to endure all that mess. I just felt we had a connection. Reality can be a bitch because he wasn't on the same page. He was more invested in a group plan, not funny. Doc did say the words, it sounds genuine, and it was more than three times. It resorted back to the bad divorce, so bad that it was still bothering him ten years later — the wall to protect his heart, two children, ex-wife, and child support. I held him up, and he did not have to ask, so no fuck returns.

Did we talk about marriage? No, we never talk about marriage as in he and I. He made comments or asked a question, would you travel the country with me in an RV going to Basketball games? Would you be satisfied in a small house with two bedrooms? I responded back, yes, as long as you are there I would.

Self-Therapy if you can recall from our conversation last night, I can do a lot of things. I don't turn to negative things, and I know the outcome won't be good, so no drugs, alcohol, or activities unbecoming of a lady. So, it usually is something that I can do when I retire or make money from on the side. It works for me, I did go to a therapist once, but it was family-related when my mother died. All the techniques she told me how to use I already knew to do. However, sometimes you just need that non-judgmental ear. It is hard when you are going through it, and no one is there to listen to you, and I haven't had that until this year. Andrea offers great advice, told me to leave him alone that he is not good for me, but she understood my feelings, and with her advice, I was still going to follow my heart with what I felt I needed to do. Self-worth is big to me because I know mine, I saw more in him than he saw of himself. We can talk about it (yes, Jimmy, I will be willing, if someone showed interest). I read something of the sort years ago on the different types of love, just as you did.

Well, yes, I agree, we meet because of our love for writing, and as I see it from my perspective, you would never be a follow-up. Building a foundation is the most important part of any relationship, firm ground to stand upon. Please, tell me about the Ashford and Simpson type of love. Because you sending the pic's does not put us in that zone. I am good since it's been a good while, not telling you how long. Yet, I can wait, and we do small things like hold hands, lol, but both may be a better deal because I want that solid as a rock thing to friendship and love that strong as steel relationship.

If you want me to know you more, sharing something new with me every day or week is a good start. I thought: Jimmy seems as if he is a gentleman, sweet, kind, and polite on the first day I meet you. I like your smile, how your voice sounds when you talk to me, I check out your feet and fingers, wow, those fingers. My thoughts of you are of high regard. You can be "my person" I would love for you to be my person if you have that spark...burning on fire interested. I am not just being sweet and polite; you are what I want. I asked an old woman once, how do you know when you have met your person. She said you would feel it, and I am feeling it now.

Aww, that is so sweet. I am flattered. Do you think I am sort of handsome or decent on the eye? I guess I possess a few attributes you're attracted to. I want you to get to know as much about me as possible. I rather know upfront. If you like, sounds like a pre-teen type of love letter. Do you like me? Check Yes or No. When I first laid eyes on you, I was looking at you like that because I was looking at it like a business meeting. I was a little nervous. I think it had something to do with your title in the union. You are very laid back, and I don't see you having a crazy bone in your body. You seem like a mellow soul. You're probably what I need in my life, too. And I don't want you being any rebound either. I don't know how much time you'd need to get over Doc and I over Ana, but I would like for us to get over them together. The more I get to know about you, the more I like you. Also, on the first day, I met you, you had a different look. I can't put my finger on it. The comedy show footage and the WSBTV archive allows me to see your facial features as often as I like. You do know men are visual, so I am always trying to see how big your ass and tits are without being too obvious.

I can tell your body is modest, but who knows what lies underclothes, but if you were thick, I'd see it block away. And as far as the pics I sent, I will agree, it doesn't mean we rushed into the fuck zone. You can be patient. So, is a 2.5-inch heel the only heel height you'll wear? I like sex appeal, but not overboard with your titties out in public. So, what is your type of man? Athletic, tall, muscular, thuggish, preppy, dreads, stocky, chubby chaser, are you?

Taller than you? Light or dark? Back to Doc, why do you think he lied? Do you now not trust long-distance relationships? As anyone at VAMC sparked interest? I prefer to say has anyone at VAMC sparked *your* interest? You have definitely sparked my interest, and I don't want to move too fast or too slow. How did my name come up with Stephanie? Would you consider her a good-good friend? If you were on a girl's trip to Jamaica and your friends cheated on their husbands or significant others, would you? Do you succumb to peer pressure? Have you ever cheated on your man? So, tell your current marital status? You told me before, but I guess as just a guy who was reading pages of your novel, I didn't retain that information.

Now I am feeling smitten? How often do you think about sex? Have you ever led a man to believe you were a sex kitten, then when you're good deep into a committed relationship, view sex as a chore or slight inconvenience? What city do you actually live in? Stephanie is a nice dresser. Do you like her style?

I definitely, do not want a man shorter than me, my height or my taller and I can work with his body image. Just not the overly muscular broad shoulders with meeting the neck type. I would wear 3-inch heels if they were wedges but 2.5 is it? Jimmy, I grew up both Baptist and Muslim, so my body is usually covered in the winter and arms in the summer dresses above the knees, no shorts. Completion does not matter, my high school sweetheart, if he went outside and it was dark you could not find him. Black Joe, in the darkness, he could be close but you would not see him.

Back to Doc, As You Requested.

I don't think he expected me to bring him lunch, and I told him there was no need for the lie. Just be honest. Of course, I still trust long-distance relationship, no doubt. This is my weeding process, getting all the weeds out of the way so I can see and my green grass grows. No one at the VA has sparked my interest, absolutely no one. Please, not too slow. Stephanie, your name came up because I was trying to get her to read a few pages, and she declined due to the feeling she would have to experience once she got home. She thought we would hit it off and probably hit it off. I would consider her good. No, I won't. I don't succumb to peer pressure, more of a loner. Cheated on my man, let me make some room for this answer.

No, I had already made the decision that he was no longer my man, for example, Doc (ended), and a second example would be Chris (ended).
When I got with Doc, I told him about my relationship with Chris. On paper, and within a month a divorce pending, and husband has only to sign his name. Yes, I am really that age, is that too old for you? Just being me, but young at heart. I go to bed much later than you. I think about sex, making love or masturbating every day just not all day. James of course, not the kitten. I live in Snellville off of why 124, ten miles from Stone Crest Mall. Yes, Stephanie is a nice dresser, and I like her style for her. But I love the colors.

Let's, finish with Doc, I just wanted to be with you!
I haven't seen Doc in six months, long heart aching months. I have only heard his voice twice, but he will text, good morning Sunshine, have a wonderful day. Good night TS rest well. To his three or four words, I would reply with paragraphs of text message and no further responses from him. I was hungry just to get those few words.

I often wondered what he was really doing or thinking. I would hope that just one day out of the week, he would call as he used to before I got married. He was short, cut off, and non-communicative for over a year, damn. I told him every time we met up that I am sorry, and it was a mistake. Yet, he had his persons, and I knew of them just did not tell him I was aware of his activities.

But I love him so much he was on my mind all day and night I began to wonder what is wrong with me. I texted him that I was going to Augusta Ga for training for work Oct 30 to Nov 1, and be visiting my sister thereafter. I called Doc before I sent the text message, but he did not respond. "Doc, why aren't you answering my calls or responding to my text?" My girlfriend said, "girl, he got someone else living with him." I responded with, "that's probably been the case for a while." I needed him just to tell me even though I already knew about the multiple women his brother told me about, and that's all he could say. Maybe he was feeling the way about using me for his needs. Shit, I believe in karma, and that shit would return to sender fast.

The three days I spent in Augusta Ga and text communication gave me a Bitch attitude. I felt like he did not want me to come. It took three days to get reservations. I tried until I was tired of trying, and I changed my password, then the Hotel system went down for maintenance. My daughter tried my niece, still no reservations. I decided to go to my sister Jennifer. Upon my arrival, I washed my laundry, did my eyelashes, ate my juicy crabs and watched a few movies, just relaxing. Around 9 p.m. Thursday night I tried once again, and everything worked. But dam, I was really feeling the block for me not to go to Charleston. My curiosity got the best of me, and I went anyway. Mind you not, I have attempted to go see him over the past six months, got within 45, 40, and 20 miles and could go no further. Because I felt he was not feeling me anymore. I needed him to just say that one thing, so I won't want to keep coming back like a hungry vampire.

October 2018 made 2 years since I have known Doc. Longest, one-night stand and only one for me. It was in my heart that I hoped he would fall in love with me, my Twin Flame, I felt the connection. But yes, there is a "if". I sent him another text message after I checked into the Hotel. He asked, "where are you? Are you still in Beaufort?" I said, "no, I am down the street at the Homewood's Suites next to our DoubleTree, where we had our first night," no further response. So, I texted again, "if you decide to, or decide not to or prefer to keep your silent movement going. I will be here until Sunday, leaving at 11:00 room 316.

In the meantime, I slept Friday, pissed off as fuck, still got up, and got him breakfast just in case he showed up. He did not show up nor text, so I enjoyed the breakfast with a fuck you smile. I watched TV in the dark and listened to Love songs while pissed off as a mother fucker. But I was still feeling some- kind- of-a- way about him possibly not wanting me to come over. I could just as easily drive 1 mile to his job. Maybe I missed the opportunity to see the man I Love, or maybe it was an opportunity to see that he does not Love me.

No contact on Friday, no contact on Saturday, I sent another text, and it read, "I hope you are okay." Still nothing, and I did not want to drive over to his apartment to start a scene. I just wanted to talk with him, and his place was only 6 miles away and his job 1 mile away.
Okay, I put myself in a rough position now he is in the fuck you fucker I am going to talk about your dick zone, not even friends. Shit, nothing I can say bad about the dick. I still love him. I expected things would be the same whenever I came to visit. He has always been available. But this was surprisingly different. Not a word.

I left an open invitation in hopes he would show. Now, it's Sunday night, and I sent no more texts, did not go by his apartment, nor called him. I went out shopping, saw a few tall, handsome men in the Hotel lobby as I was leaving heads turned in my direction, of course. I smiled, said hello, and kept walking to my car. I bought this nice lace wig; crimp curls pass my shoulder hanging mid-back. Make-up flawless glossy lip gloss with a pink tinge. I took myself to dinner, a little self-love, and talked with my girls. They asked, "girl, did he show up?" yet I said, "Nope, I don't expect him to come at this point." I checked my phone periodically to see if he had texted or called, but no.

December 2018, still nothing, but his brother gave me updates until I stopped inquiring about how he was doing. My divorce was final January 09, 2019, but I told no one, just had a little hope that he would make some sort of effort. I got a text Happy New Year, and I sent only the same in return. I wanted to say more but maintained my restraint. February 2019, sent a Happy Valentine's Day GIF, got one back in return. The next text came on Mother's Day, and I sent one for Father's Day. No happy birthday from Doc, but none expected. That feeling of Love still sitting on the top of my heart and the desire to have him and be in his arms still in my heart. Still yearning for the touch of his lips on mine and between my legs. He had all my heart, and no one else was even a good distraction. I was missing him so much. I sent him a Love song in a moment of weakness, which I apologized for, but no response. In my heart, I knew he read it and smiled. His brother would say something to me a few days later about the song. Over the next few months, I continued to send songs, and one I miss you text.

June 2019, still no real conversation, but I do believe he would see me if I went to Charleston. I am emotionally traumatized about the possibility of being rejected. Damn, that is usually not me when it comes to love I am usually bold and Dearing. It has been hard trying to let go of the

past and move on. I still want Doc, and I feel he will be
back.

Jimmy

I thought he was the One, but it wasn't really for him. Jimmy told me in March of 2019 that he wanted a break but not as in ending the relationship. I said, what and he repeated the sentence with many emotions and a shaky voice. I had never in all my years ever heard such bull shit. So, I said nonchalantly, ok. I was thinking silently and dialoguing to myself, who does this big head motherfucker think he is. He does not have it like that. We went on talking a lot in the morning, day, and the last thing in the night, just the very little communication, then nothing. Now, I know the continue minimal contact was to lighten to impact of the punch to my heart. Shit, I decided to spend more time with my ex-husband to keep my mind of these two Bitches…yes, I can say that.

Yes, he drove a nice ride. Yes, he dressed like he owned the cover of GQ Magazine. On the outside, he was what he thought he was the shit in a suit. But let me tell you he was fuck up to the max on the inside.

After a month, he texts and asks if I would be upset if he told me he was interested in someone else. What the fuck…First, the question was a little puzzling. You just told me I was better to you than your four wives put together. You would buy me a ring, but you don't have any money. So, dialoguing with myself once again, I am going to talk about this mother fucker's dick. There is plenty I can say about his dick. I try not to hurt his feelings and think before

I speak. But in my mind, I am angry as fuck and giving no more fucks to fuck boy. However, with a smile in my voice, I said no I wouldn't be upset, follow your heart I can't make you love me thanks for letting me know.

As the weeks past, we would send meaningless, mostly text messages, but the undertone was I have a lot to say to you, motherfucker, but I am not going to give you the pleasure. You will miss me more than I miss you, and I got the lesson this time — no more repeats. Yeah, your dick is big, and I appreciate you not wanting to stretch my little pussy. I really thank you for not wanting to ruin me for the next man.

This mother fucker was a lot of work. I have got to stop fixing broken useless men. That think sex is love or is the number one priority. I thought he had potential, potential that I thought that he was a good man and deserved to be loved in the best way possible, and the start was amazing. Yet, he was still stuck on wife number two, Ana. What bets me to this day. Even after he told me the story of what he wanted from her; I was still wondering why.

I told him she is giving you your answer without saying the words you want to hear. It sounds a lot like my story right I know. Right this moment, June 27, 2019, at 3:47 p.m., it is clear that Doc is my Ana, same treatment. Jimmy posts on Facebook June 10th, 2019, that "she said yes, I saw the picture of the women, and I thought it was his mother or older sister that was saying yes to a proposal, so I give a thumbs up.

I guess that wasn't enough, so he posted again, and again, and again way into the next day the same shit. By now, I realized it was their engagement, for a few brief seconds, it dawned on me that I hurt. It lasted over the weekend, then he posted a picture of him and her together, and I could not believe my eyes. My second thought was he must be doing this to get back at Ana but you would need something that appeared better on the outside. You see, he like a thick woman about 6'2 to 6'5 inches tall and about 200 pounds shapely. Shit, I am 5'9" and 175 pounds and all legs.

I evaluated our relationship and something in the milk wasn't clean, it doesn't add up. Her skills can't be that racked up. I decided to give him a run, player, I was going to peek his cards. Is it the sex? Well, I made a move and showed I was still interested. We talked on the phone more, Skype during working hours, had talks after word and said good night every day. We went to a few shows but only if he did the inviting so I let him. Things were going to be different this time I wasn't going overboard. My friends were advising me to not feed his ass, don't spend any time with him he needs to be alone…just fuck him. I don't have that type of blood running in my veins, I am the nice girl.
He was feeling guilty about our rejoining and heighten emotional connection. I was sweet, loving, attentive, a good listen and up my romance game. I made sure my make up was flawless and my best attribute stood out, my lips. He enjoyed looking at my lips as much as a fat ass woman. I wanted a real game changer so I asked questions, for instance, "can I bring over my little toy?" I think you will like it; I promise to be gentle. Never used it on him before,

but I am good with it. I brought over four in my little black bag but I only used one, but not until two months later. During the first two months it was just kissing, a lot of sensuous deep throat kissing and a lot of moaning. He had forgotten how well I lips danced together like two ballerinas. He said, damn has your kisses always been like that, I smiled and turned to look him straight in the eye. Yes Babe, our kisses have always been electrifying. I got wet and he got hard. I am listening to his body talk to me.

Jimmy, said he doesn't like all the kissing all over, just get straight to the point. That's what I did the first round, now I am going to do it my way. So, I got the kiss…and I am going to work three spots at one time. He has some nice nipples, perfectly erect and a prime target spot for nibbling. So, I nibble gently and held his nipple between my teeth while I stroke his oily dick. Nice response. Babe, was that too hard? No, it was the perfect combination of pleasure and pain. So, I told Jimmy I wanted him to get to know me because he did not give us that chance. So, I will spend time with you but I can't let you go down town no licking, sucking, or smelling. We were going to practice safe sex and it would be amazing without penetration. So, for two months, it was just kissing, showering together, kissing, nipple bites and rim jobs. He really was turned on by the rim jobs. Nipple biting and a rimmy he was calling me to come or stop at his home first on my way home on Wednesday. I work out of State, three days of the week and I usually get back to town by 7 p.m.

I would stop at his home for the night. He would have dinner ready, salmon with cream Alfredo sauce, mixed vegetable melody and a glass of red wine. Perfectly, wonderful change. Yes, he is still engaged but I felt in my heart he wasn't in love with her. So, I shared that fact with him. Furthermore, I was blunt with another fact. As Jimmy satin his favorite leopard arm chair in the living room, after our romantic candle light dinner I suggested we talk. He was cool with having a conversation, there was time because he likes to be in bed by 10 p.m. can't deter from that schedule. I would like to share my observation with you with regards to your relations to include ours.

He took a sip of the wine, crossed his legs and nodded his head for me to proceed. Babe, just listen carefully firstly I love you and that hasn't change. You are my person you just don't know it yet. If I believed you are in love with her, I would not be here and you would not have me here. I think you made a drastic move to make Ana jealous and it backfired. So, now you are invested and think you can't get out. Please, stop me if I am wrong. Shasha, I have invested a lot of money and time, her family and friends are expecting us to get married. I have been trying to get a job in Florida but it's not working out. Yes, I can hear your voice, it's not time or meant to be. God moves you when he wants and not when you want. Maybe you have more work to do in Atlanta or help your kids out. Jimmy I will be with you until June 8, 2020 depending on what decision you make. I hear you talking but I hear nothing about you or love only investment. Investments fail every day, look at the stock market. Jimmy, Babe…happiness is important and love even more-so. Don't save face because of friends and family and end up divorcee in a year. Then you would have missed out on me. I may not be your choice later, and you may realize before July she isn't either, I just want you to make the best decision for you.

On that note, we can go to bed. I went upstairs to shower while he washed the dishes. I moved slowly, so he could join me in the shower later. I wanted him to rub my pussy with the soapy clothe as I propped my left leg up and rest it on the side of the tub. He likes to play with my bush, so I don't dare cut a strain. His hand moves back and forth with a soothing motion with the hot soapy cloth gliding across my clit it was so stimulating my pussy tighten up as he slides that one finger I love inside. I grabbed his hand and pressed it firmly against my pussy lips, now his hand engulfed all of me. We kissed and creased under the steamy hot water until I pulled his dick towards me...that was two-hands pull. I bathe him down for all the spots I was going to visit, once we hit that bed. Damn, he looks good, all that long tall dark chocolate and I going to suck it all up. I love how his body responds... he gets so aroused as my hands and mouth work him over from head to toe. Shasha, come on over here and get your dick, it's pointing in your direction babe, come on. I climb in the bed from the foot, and straddle his body as I come on his lips.

I listen for the noise of his moans and groans as or tongues wrestle and my juicy pussy rest on top of his stomach, he is warm enough for a little oily rub down and I am wet enough for the finger. I switch positions and move to his side, but he keeps that finger in place. Forefinger in pussy thrusting in and out meeting the thumb and the little man in the boat. I spread my legs wider, his finger went deeper and I let out a long sigh as I call his name, Jimmy oh babe, right there. I bend over from his right side and give him a few nibbles as I stroke that massive long hard dick. I wasn't going to give him any head but the dick looked so good I just had to wrap my full lips around my chocolate delight. Jimmy calls out my name, Shasha, oh Shasha I have been craving the touch of your mouth touching my dick, that first touch is electrifying. Suck your dick, suck your dick and his voice elevates, SUCK YOUR DICK. I take it all the way down and to the back of my throat. I could hear in his screams how much pleasure he was experiencing. Thank you, Babe, thank you!

I decided to introduce him to my little friend, the bullet. The bullet was short, slim, purple and filled with power. With my thighs spread apart I am still on my knees, I said relax Babe I got you. I suck his dick, sloppy for I a few more minutes letting the salvia run down the sides of my hands. I took my powerful toy and placed it right under his balls, all that high vibrating was better than sucking his dick and humming. I did not want the dick to get cold so I sucked for a while longer. My god it was intense for him and exhilarating for me to be able to take him there. The more I sucked his dick the wetter my pussy became. It was like Niagara Falls a continue flow of juices. Damn Shasha, your pussy is so wet. Thank God for long arms, for a long reach I was able to hold the vibrator in place, give him a one hand rimmy and nibble in the nipples. The more I bit harder the louder the noise escalated. I bit and chew and rubbed and stroked until he said lay down. I laid on my back and he turned the lights up. He like watching me play with my clit, I give him hat visual stimulation. Legs spread like an eagle in flight I wanted him to see it all, I watched is dick grow longer with each stroke. He was almost ready to explode, and I wasn't finish with Jimmy yet. I wanted to milk him to the last drop, so I played with my pussy with my little purple toy as he watched my clit plump up and I gasp for air. Jimmy was ready so I placed my little purple toy under his balls...the feeling was none he had felt before...but damn I knew it was good to him. He started to Cumming, and Cumming and Cumming all over my breast. He doesn't know where he wants to go because I am not turning the dick loose. I milked it and milked it, sprayed more oil and stroked it, put it in my mouth and sucked it, until nothing was left. He rolled over off of his knees and just laid there for a few minutes. I asked, him Babe are you okay? He was holding his head and shaking his head...I placed a hot towel on his dick for a few seconds, then I cleaned him up and gave him a little kiss on his bottom lip. I cleaned up and crawled in bed next to him. Babe, are you sure you are okay? Yes, and yes, I just keep seeing these blue lights.

About the Author

Mercuries Ryzen was born in Brooklyn, New York, and reared in the Low-Country of South Carolina. Currently, she resides in Atlanta, Ga. She is a graduate of Argosy University with a Bachelor's degree in Psychology and a Master's degree in Professional Counseling. She continues to pursue her education as she is working on her Ph.D. in Psychology and her Master's in Human Resource Management. Whenever faced with a challenge, she looked to find an area within her to work on.

After all the Psychological training, she was aware when a need for an outlet was necessary. So, Mercuries searched and found something more reasonable and affordable than a Therapist. Comedy was ideal, she wrote her routines practice in front of complete strangers and performed on stage at the Punchline in Atlanta, Georgia. That was a positive resolution for her because she was shy and completing out of her comfort zone. It is a wonderful feeling to write about your feelings, act them out on stage, and not give a damn about what others are thinking. She performs every blue moon at Open Mic night. However, another challenge raised, and that experience led to her taking a Voice over class, which was intriguing in itself to act out another side of her personality.

Mercuries is a career nurse and has been with her current employer for 29 years. She has a love for writing and her big family. She started writing at a young age and had her first poem published at the age of 12 years old. Writing is her passion and emotional outlet. She writes for the reader to feel the emotions and be part of the story. Mercuries, released her first book in 2009, "When My Soul Cries," and plans to release her novel in November 2019. "Shared Tenderness" was supposed to be the title, but Men in My Bed just was a better fit. This story is designed to ensure readers that although we may have a man, or two, or three in our life. There could be unpredictable turnouts, such as none of them measuring up, younger or older, and playing games, mentally challenged. Flaccid dicks, just a Crocker sack full of shit. Therefore, we have to have the tools necessary to successfully put the pieces together to navigate and build our desired man. And good luck with that. In my writing, I want the reader to view the positive aspects of exploring numerous options and possibly recycling the man.

MR.

\\\

Made in United States
Orlando, FL
14 July 2022

19753654R00136